Sacrifice

& OTHER SHORT STORIES

Edward Eremugo Kenyi

A Note from the Publisher

The publisher wishes to acknowledge and thank Dr Douglas H. Johnson for his invaluable help and support for Africa World Books and its mission of preserving and promoting African cultural and literary traditions and history. Dr Johnson and fellow historians have been instrumental in ensuring that African people remain connected to their past and their identity. Africa World Books is proud to carry on this mission.

© Edward Eremugo Kenyi, 2020

ISBN: 978-0-6488415-8-6 (book)
ISBN: 978-0-6488415-1-7 (e-book)

Design and typesetting: Africa World Books

To my father who saw
what I could do,
my mum for being there for me and
my wife, Poni,
for her tireless support

EDWARD KENYI is a South Sudanese public health physician, poet and short story writer. His short stories have appeared in *Warscapes*, *The Kalahari Review*, the McSweeney's 43 Issue *There is a Country: New Fiction From the New Nation of South Sudan* and on Author-me.com.

Publication history of some of the short stories

Although some of the stories are originals and unpublished, majority were already published elsewhere online and in anthologies.

The Dream in Kalahari Review – January 17, 2017

Escape in the *Warscapes* anthology Literary Sudans: An Anthology of Literature from Sudan and South Sudan – October 3, 2016

Independence Day in *Warscapes* – July 11, 2016

Escape in the McSweeney's Anthology There Is a Country: New Fiction from the New Nation of South Sudan – May 7, 2013

Casualty in *Warscapes* – December 12, 2012

Meeting Mama in Author-me.com

Cousins in Author-me.com

Sacrifice in Author-me.com

Contents

I
———

Sacrifice

THE MOBILE PHONE KEPT RINGING. LODULE LOOKED AT THE PHONE screen, but the incoming number was unknown, not listed in his phonebook. He ignored it. There was a number that kept pestering him in the past few weeks. A male voice always would ask for a "Mohammed" every time he answered. He kept telling him that he was not Mohammed or anyone close enough, but to no avail. He then decided to ignore the number whenever it called. He looked at the number again when it rang for the umpteenth time. Lodule chose to answer this time.

"Hello," Lodule said, not knowing who was calling him.

"Lodule, this is Wani," a voice answered.

"Oh, how are you? Whose number are you using?"

"Lodule, there had been an accident. I hit a woman with the car, an older woman who is now in a critical condition. Come quickly."

"Where are you? How did it happen?"

"We are at the junction of Street 15 in Amarat, near the petrol station. Come quickly please, I am using someone's phone, and he needs it back."

"I know the place. I am quite near and am on my way."

Lodule sprang from his desk at the shop in Souk al Shaabi Khartoum, the vast market in Khartoum South, and ran outside. He had a small business there that had seen better days. His assistant from Darfur, who people came to refer to as the Al Darfuri, had gone out for coffee. Outside, Lodule called out the man, and he came from behind the kiosk where he had been taking his coffee.

"I am going out to Amarat," he said. "My brother had an accident, and I am going there. Look after the place."

Lodule walked to the nearby street and hailed an Amjad minibus taxi.

"Street 15," he told the driver. He did not even bother to ask how much. He can't afford to haggle over the cost of the journey. There was no time. What the man asked later, he would pay.

When he got there, a crowd had gathered at the place. A small group assembled in one corner of the junction, looking at someone seated on the ground. From the look of it, the police had not arrived yet. It was curious onlookers who were crowding around. Lodule hurried on to see. Wani sat on the curb, his head buried in his hands. Lodule moved the people aside and sat next to him. He put his arms around him. When Wani raised his eyes, they were swollen, reddish. He had been crying.

"They took her to the Khartoum Hospital," he said, between sobs. "I do not have a driving license. What will I do? What will happen to me?"

Lodule's nightmare had come to pass. His most dreaded fear had occurred. Wani had always been driving in Khartoum. He learned driving when he was very young, indeed. He had grown up in Mayo slums, where he worked as a turn-boy on a bus for an Arab businessman.

He learned to drive and was allowed at night to transport passengers on his own, even though he had no driving license. It is no surprise, though. In Khartoum, many people drive without the right papers. If you got caught in one of the numerous random police checks, you only have to pay the fine or bribe your way out of it, and you go free. The problem would be when you had an accident, like what Wani was facing.

The minibus he was driving still parked in the middle of the road. Traffic had to pass around it. As in many accidents, the car remained in its place until the police mapped the accident.

"Look here, bro," Lodule said. "Be calm. I will handle the situation. I will say I was driving because I have a license. Everything will be all right. You are lucky the crowd did not beat you up."

"But they will know it was not you," he argued.

"Don't worry, just be calm. Let us go over there and wait." Lodule picked him up and moved away from the crowd.

A few minutes later, a police car pulled up by the side of the road. Its blue and red lights flashing, but the siren was off. Two policemen came out of the car and walked over to where Lodule and Wani were seated. One of the people still lingering around had pointed them out to the policemen. Lodule stood up when he saw them approaching.

"Who was driving the car," one of them asked. The man was a mean-looking fellow. His clothes were shabby like he had been sleeping in them. He must be having a rough day.

"I am," Lodule said confidently.

"Can I have your driving license, please," he ordered.

Lodule pulled out his wallet from the back pocket of his trousers and fished out the driving license. Although he had no car, he always carried it with him. The driving license had served him well, as he could use it as an ID. He did not have the national ID card. Ever since it expired four years ago, he had never bothered himself to renew it. The license worked just fine.

The policeman checked the license and looked up at him to verify that the picture was indeed his. Satisfied, he put it in his breast pocket.

"Where is the vehicle registration?" he wanted to know. The other policeman was already by the side of the car, examining the screech marks on the tarmac.

"In the car," Lodule said.

Lodule walked self-assuredly over to the car. He was not sure where to find it or whether he would even find it. He had only the faintest idea where it could be. He had seen where many drivers kept their vehicle registration papers. The car keys were still in the ignition. He opened the driver's side and looked into the pocket on the dashboard. It was not there. He pulled down the sun visor over the driver's view. Stacked in a role were some papers. He pulled them out and spread them on the seat. He looked through them and found it buried between the documents. He handed it to the policeman. The policeman looked at the papers carefully.

"It expired yesterday, my friend," he said, his face breaking into a sardonic smile as if he was pleased with the find. "You are in deep trouble."

Lodule just looked at him. The expression on his face betrayed nothing. It is a simple mishap. Maybe, they will overlook, since it was only a day old.

"I was actually on my way to renew it," he lied.

"Tell that to the judge," the policeman replied. "You must come with us to the station so that we record your statement. After that, we shall come back here to verify the accident and draw it."

"I will go with you," Wani said. He looked much calmer, much himself, not the sobbing little man.

"Never mind, take my phone and call home," Lodule whispered to him in Arabi Juba, the common form of Arabic used by South Sudanese, so that the policemen would not know what he was saying. "Don't stay around too much. Tell them what happened. I shall meet them at the police station. And don't come with them, please. You should keep away from the police station."

The police station was bustling with activity. When they got to the building, the officers took Lodule to a desk where a man registered his particulars. He also narrated how the accident happened. Most of it was guesswork since he was not there. They recorded everything as he told them. In the end, the desk officer told him he would be remanded in custody until the prosecutor came by to post bail. He will review the case and decide on the bail amount.

The officers took everything from his pockets. They handed them over to the desk police officer who painstakingly recorded every piece of item: his wallet, two mobile phones for different networks, the car keys, pen, belt, and the gold necklace. He was especially poignant at having to give away this priced possession. He had never taken the chain off from the time when he bought it four years previously. It had always adorned his long neck. Now he had to part with it as he went into custody. He wondered whether he would ever see these things again. The police officer stashed everything into a large khaki envelope and stapled it. He wrote his name across the back and put it on a shelf behind him.

One policeman led Lodule to the cell. The holding cell at the police station was no bigger than a bedroom. It had the feel of a fish market, and the foul stench emanating from inside through the grated steel door was a mixture of sweat, dust, and urine. He fished out a bunch of keys, like the proverbial jailer he was, and opened the door. Lodule walked inside, and he locked the door behind him. The inside was damp like the toilet with no entries. The many people inside were crowding near the door as if they were gasping for air. He found a corner, squatted, and began the long wait.

The prosecutor came late in the evening when he had already given up hope. His family had not arrived yet. He wondered where Wani was. He could be anywhere, trying to locate his mother in Mayo area and get some friends and uncles. He would do that, that boy. Since he knew quite well that Lodule is inside instead of him, he thought. Wani remained the only brother Lodule had. Their mother raised them when they were still very young in the slums of Mayo, brewing illegal alcohol to make ends meet. Their father, a well-known drunkard of the first degree, had died. He was found dead at the door to his own home. The coroner had told them that he died from severe alcohol hangover, a condition locally referred to as ketuk. Their mother took care of them all this time. They grew strong together as inseparable siblings playing football in the slums. They have also participated in some mischief together. Wani had been his brother and friend. That was why it came quickly to him to bail him out of his predicament.

A police officer called him, breaking his reverie, and led him to a small office at the back of the cell. He found a smartly dressed young man, with a white shirt and blue tie sitting behind a narrow desk. In front of him were heaps of papers he was reading. Without looking up, he motioned to Lodule to sit down on the metal chair in front of the desk. The police officer stood behind him after handing over another piece of paper.

"What is your name," the prosecutor asked. The man was very young for the job. It was like he had just passed his bar and coming in here to practice. He wore a striped tie on a white shirt. He had no coat. His complexion was fair and looked as if he had a fresh haircut. The hairline was sharp like that of a marine corp.

"Lodule," he answered.

"Foursome please, Rubayi," the young prosecutor said, raising his voice louder.

"Julius Lodule Carlo Bambu," Lodule replied.

"Age?"

"30"

"Residence?"

"Mayo, Tawidad."

"I know Mayo, but where is the Tawidad?"

"It is part of the new extensions of Mayo, southwards, near the canals."

"What are you in here for?"

Lodule knew very well that the attorney had all the information. The fact that they were cross-examining him like he was a murderer was about to get into his nerves. After all, it was just a bloody car accident, he thought.

"A car accident," he answered, trying hard to keep his voice down. He knew very well than to irk the people of the law. They could slam one with some ridiculous charges, and you would rot in jail for the rest of your life.

"It said here in the hospital report that her condition is critical. The bail will be set high, at fifty thousand pounds. As the case stands, you will pay all the expenses for her treatment in the hospital. If she recovered fully, there would be a hearing in front of the judge."

Lodule gave a long sigh of relief. The bail terms were acceptable, as long as he had his freedom. He could not afford to go back into the dingy cell.

"We will impound the car until someone pays the insurance and the necessary fines," he continued.

Lodule was not listening. His mind was already preoccupied with the issue of the money. From where will they get such an amount within a short time?

"You can go," he added.

The prosecutor signed some papers and handed them over to the police officer standing near the door. He took them and opened the door. Lodule walked out, and the officer followed to the desk.

"You will get your belongings once you make the payment," the

SACRIFICE & OTHER SHORT STORIES

officer behind the counter said.

Lodule was led back into the cell. Just then, he heard some commotion and moved to the door. His neighbor Tombe had arrived with an entourage. There was his mother too.

"Are you OK, did they do something to you? Did they beat you?" his mother started asking. Her voice was hesitant; the tone bore a sad feeling to it. She had been crying, he could tell.

"Nothing Mama, I am fine," Lodule answered.

"What happens next? Will you go home?"

"Yes. The attorney set bail of one thousand pounds because the old woman is in critical condition."

"Do not worry. We have already spoken to your uncle Daniel," his mother said. "He is coming soon, with some money."

Lodule's mother was looking terrible. She had been crying, Lodule could tell. Her eyes were swollen and scarlet red. The long multi-colored flowing tobe she wore was dangling and trailing on the ground, collecting dust from the dirty floor. She never seemed to mind.

Presently, uncle Daniel came waddling into the waiting area. He was a heavy man, grossly overweight, with a round face with deep black eyes that seem to penetrate inside the thing he was watching. He had the habit of looking you square in the eyes without blinking when speaking. It could be disconcerting sometimes.

"How are you," he asked, not addressing anyone in particular, his eyes darting from Tombe, mother and back to Lodule, who was still holding on to the metal grates of the cell.

"There is a bail of one thousand. Do you have it?" Lodule's mother asked.

"Yes, I have enough money with me."

"You can pay over there, at the counter."

Uncle Daniel ambled off to pay the bail. Shortly he came back to the door with a policeman who opened the door, and Lodule walked out. He marched to the desk where he found a different man than the one who had taken his possessions. The man gave Lodule a paper to sign and handed the khaki envelop with his name on it. He opened it and pulled out his things. The gold chain was missing.

"I have a gold chain. It is no longer here."

"Are you sure," the officer asked. "Let me check the records."

He pulled out the big book, marked "Records" in big Arabic letters, and opened it. He flipped to the pages. The officer read it silently and looked up.

"There is no mention of a gold chain in these records," the officer said.

Lodule was startled. How could his gold chain disappear just like that, off the records? He was sure he saw the other officer noting it down.

"Are you sure this was the correct record book? I saw him write it down."

"It is not here," the man said. "If you have any complaints, you will need to file a case for the missing gold chain. Other than that, I can't help you."

Lodule felt as if the world had shrunk. His heart started beating faster and faster like a drum gone wild, and his face broke into sweats, tiny little drops that cascaded all over his body. He had lost his most prized possession of many years. The way the officer spoke, he knew he would never set his eyes on it again.

"Let us go," his mother said. "You will find another one. It is good that you are out of this place."

Lodule followed them outside. The sun had already gone down as darkness took over. The street lights were like pools of color, sprayed from a large-bored hose on the ground.

The family decided to visit the woman in the hospital. She was in the intensive care unit. The family of the woman met Lodule, his mother, and uncle Daniel. The daughter of the woman was seated on a mattress in the veranda of the ICU. She was crying. Maybe the outcome was not that good, he thought. When she saw them approached, the young lady stood up and shouted at them.

"You murderers," she cried. "You almost killed my mother. What are you coming here to do? Are you coming to laugh at us?"

She lashed out at Lodule, who was closer to her. She hit him square on the face, and his head spun as if a hammer hit him. A man standing close by jumped up and restrained the lady, struggling to calm her down.

"You better leave," he said. "Please, we will talk later."

The man seemed reasonable and understanding. As a group, they backed out of the room. The experience shocked Lodule, a bad sign indeed.

"It would have been better if we had not come at all," Lodule's mother said. "Look at how they treated you."

"It is understandable, mama," Lodule said. "They are still in shock at what happened. They will understand later."

The knock at the door was deafening. It was not even six o'clock yet. The cold November morning had winds crushing on the corrugated iron roofs, making hissing sounds that resembled a snake in the bushes. Lodule struggled to get up from his bed. His body was still aching from the troubled week he had been going through. He had not even been to the business in Souk al Shaabi market. Things have not been going fine for him. The costs of treatment for the lady in the hospital kept rising. The demands kept coming, and he just wished everything would end soon. He got up from his bed and sauntered outside, still sleepy-eyed. He struggled to open the gate. Two police officers stood outside. A patrol car parked some distance on the opposite side of the road looked occupied. The full moon was just setting in the west, giving faint light that reflected off the shiny linings of the car. A man in plain cloth spoke first.

"Are you Lodule?" he asked.

"Yes, I am. What is this about?" Lodule asked.

"The woman whom you hit with the car died last night. The attorney had left a standing order to bring you in if anything happens to the woman."

"How did it happen? She was quite well the last time we visited?"

"That is not for me to tell. I am no doctor. All I know is that she is dead. You are coming with us. Get dress properly."

Up this moment, Lodule did not realize that he was in the boxer shorts that he wore yesterday. The white T-shirt he wore was thin, and he started to feel the cold. When he rushed back inside, Wani and his mother were awake.

"What is it Lodule?" his mother asked. She came out of her room after hearing Lodule opened the gate. She was still in her nightdress. She wiped her eyes and looked at the Lodule.

"The police. The woman had died. They want me back at the station."

"Oh, my God. God have mercy. What can we do now, my son?" She started to cry again.

Lodule held his mother for a few minutes. He could not believe that the whole story would come to this, that the woman would die. And this has now complicated the entire case. He put on faded jeans over his boxers and picked his shirt from the hanger by the window. He went outside, and his mother and Wani followed. The police officer grabbed his arms and led him to the patrol car.

"Where are you taking him?" his mother asked.

"To the police station in Khartoum II," one of the officers replied.

"Get me a lawyer," Lodule said, turning to speak to Wani as they shoved into the vehicle.

"Why did you insist that it was you who hit the old woman," the lawyer asked.

Lodule thought they found a good lawyer for him. Bambu was a good lawyer, but Lodule thought he was asking the wrong questions now. He should try to get him out of the predicament he was in, instead of focusing on who should have been in the dock. When they took him back that day, he spent the whole day behind bars, waiting for the attorney to come. However, being Friday, he was not expected at all. Lodule spent the night in jail. The attorney came the following morning to hear the cases. He scheduled Wani to appear before the criminal judge at the court in Khartoum.

The judge heard the case and Lodule was found guilty of manslaughter, reckless driving and having a car without insurance and license. For these issues, the court fined him one hundred thousand pounds. The manslaughter charge remains. The family had refused the blood money and asked for the death penalty. Their lawyer insisted he had evidence that the driver hit the woman deliberately, thus, meaning a deliberate accident. The judge adjourned the hearing until the witnesses appear before him.

"I was doing it for my brother. I wanted to save him from the problem of the license."

"That was a stupid thing to do."

"I never knew it would come to this."

"The judge had it wrong. A traffic accident does not warrant a death penalty. We will launch an appeal. We will talk about that when the time comes."

A few days later, Bambu came back to visit Lodule at the Kobar prison, where he was awaiting the trial. He sat with him at the visitors' corner, where many other people were visiting relatives who were in jail. He had a very distant look and seemed to be carrying a heavy load in his heart.

"What is it today, Bambu?" Lodule broke the ice after a long time spent looking at the table. A lady making tea in the compound brought them two steaming cups of strong, black Sudanese coffee. It filled the crowded place with the sweet smell of heavily spiced coffee.

"It is not good news," Bambu said. "You are up against some formidable opponents. The accident had turned nasty, my friend. What I found out was that the family had great connections in the government, and one relative is a minister. They are up to get you hanged. They paid judged off already, and they are bringing false witnesses to prove that it was no accident. It is getting more complicated."

"I know this kind of people," Lodule answered. He was shocked at the turn of events and how the other side was portraying it. They have turned it into a racial and religious issue, a Southerner versus a Northerner, the Kafir and infidel versus the Muslim. It did get nasty all right, he thought.

"There is no way we are going to win this case."

"We can appeal."

"Yes, it will buy more time, but what else? They control the system, my friend."

"So, what are you saying?"

"There is the option of claiming mental problems. It will at least lead to the commutation of the charge to life in prison."

"I am not mentally disturbed," Lodule barked. "How can you say that?" His voice rose every time. The other people sitting around him looked up and went back to their talks.

"Calm down. Your family hired me to save your neck. That is what I am trying to do. It may sound weird, but is a legal loophole to hold on to."

"I don't know what to say," Lodule answered, his voice now subdued.

Bambu got up and picked his briefcase. He at looked Lodule and walked towards the door.

"I will be back soon. Take care of yourself."

When the judge came into the chamber, everybody rose. He sat on the high table, and everybody else sat down. Everyone was there. Lodule was brought into the court room handcuffed and made to stand in the holding area behind bars. The family of the woman was sitting on the right side, subdued, but unrelenting.

The arguments have already been done several times in the previous court appearances. The woman's lawyer had presented witnesses who claimed that they saw the driver swerved to hit the woman intentionally. One even claimed that he knew Lodule because he worked with him before. He said he had grudges against the family.

Bambu presented his client as an innocent man who was going about his business and got involved in a car accident, which could happen to anyone. He insisted it was not premeditated, as the driver did not know the victim, or of her family. It was sad the lady died, but it was an accident. Pure and simple. The court rejected Bambu's earlier request that his client was mentally unstable. They did not even try to petition the client to be examined by a doctor. They are not awaiting the final verdict.

"How is Wani doing?" Lodule asked.

"He is taking it very hard. He wanted to come, but we told him to keep away. He still did not know what you just told us?"

"I did not tell him anything. You are the first people to know of it."

Lodule's family had come to visit him at the prison. His friend and lawyer, Bambu, his mother, and uncle Daniel, were all there. Bambu was silent. He got up from the table and paced around. Lodule's mother and uncle Daniel sat there, listening without saying a word. The visitors' place was exceptionally empty that day. The usual horde had diminished. The emptiness was eerie and weird, as the hot afternoon weather kept many people at home. The single fan turning in the ceiling could barely cool the place.

"Why do you want to do it this way?"

"I have no choice. I don't think I have much longer to live. Let my brother have the chance."

The high court rejected all appeals, and the sentence remained that Lodule is to hang. The family of the victim was thrilled, while Lodule's family wailed and cried. The court set a date for the execution.

"Wani is my brother, my twin brother," Lodule said. "Nobody apart from us could guess that he was the true driver. I am doing it for him."

"You could have a chance too, the diagnosis could be wrong, there could be a cure, and some things may change. You can't throw your life like that."

"Whatever happened, it will still be within the family, a loss in the family. I don't have a future anymore."

Lodule's family was still in shock at the news he was telling them. They could not believe that he had been suffering silently, alone, all this time. The fact that he was dying was more shocking. Lodule told me that he had cancer of the stomach. The doctors said it was late-stage and gave him a few months to live. His symptoms had been troubling him for a long time with bouts of diarrhea and constipation. Many doctors gave him drugs that only relieved the symptoms briefly. When he started losing weight, his doctor became alarmed and referred him for an endoscopy that revealed an abnormal growth in his stomach. A biopsy showed it to be a cancerous growth. Subsequent body scans revealed spread all over the body. An operation would not benefit him.

"I am ready to give up my life for my brother," Lodule added. "I will take his place to the end. There is no going back now."

Lodule's mother stood up and came to stand beside his son. She took him in his arms as tears flowed down her cheeks, wetting Lodule's back. Her loud sobs echoed through the empty room, reverberating off the damp walls, and venturing through the windows into the corridors of the prison. She cried her heart out until she went limp and collapsed to the ground.

"Lodule, you are my blood," she said, between sobs. "You were the one who was going to look after me when I get old. Your father died when you were children. I had high hopes for you. Now you want to leave me. I will certainly die."

"Mama, please," Lodule started to say, but could not continue. He, too, was consumed by grief and the colossal decision he had taken. From the outset, it looked so unnatural, so weird. But Lodule knew deep inside him that it is the road that he would have to take.

On Monday, January first, the country was waking up to an Independence Day celebration. The new national flags were flying high in the early morning winter breeze. The president was to address a mass rally at Green Square in Khartoum at ten o'clock. There would be a military parade with fly-over by the air force. The small TV at the prison reception area was playing and showing nationalistic songs and black and white pictures of the founding fathers and the Republican Palace. At precisely five o'clock, Lodule was led to the gallows inside Kobar prison, while his twin brother Wani in Mayo was consumed by remorse and self-chastisement at the weight of the sacrifice his brother had made.

2

Meeting Mama

THE CLIMB UP THE HILL IS VERY EXHAUSTING. MY BREATHING increases, and my heart beats faster and faster. I sit on the small black, smooth-topped rock on the mountain. I take gulps of air to soothe me down. The weather is beautiful and bright this morning, as the sun rises from behind the distant mountains. They are called the Lokikili Mountains, after the tribe living there. Mama told me stories about them once. Lokikili people. They are warriors, just like our neighboring tribe, who also live in the mountains close to us. When there is fighting, they are said to be fierce and agile on their feet. Now things have changed. There are no more spears and arrows, only guns.

From here, I can see the whole village spread out in the valley like a vast carpet with a spectrum of colors on them. It is like those carpets brought from overseas. Mama used to say the rugs come from far away, across the sea, and through the forest to the village. The carpets were different from the ones our village people made from papyrus. Those were more colorful and thicker. The Arab merchants who had shops in the village brought them. Now they are all gone. They left because of the war.

Far out on the horizon are the green fields, and those are where we have the farms. It is where the groundnuts and maize are growing. I can also see part of the area where we plant the potatoes and other vegetables. The rains have been generous this year. The harvest will be okay. It is everyone's prayer. Last year the rains stopped before anyone could harvest anything. The crops were all burnt by the sun in the fields. Maybe it is a blessed year this time around.

To my left are the dark yellow roofs of the thatched huts. Strangely enough, there are not many houses with corrugated iron roofs in the village. There is only one. And that belongs to the chief. I cannot see the house from my vantage point. Chief Oluma's house is hidden behind the mango trees by the river on the other side of the village. Maybe because he is the village chief, his home is different.

Oluma. He is a funny chief. He likes to joke with people on the road. When he goes around, he moves with his Bazingili, the man who carries his whip. I remembered one time before the war, my friends and I met him on the path to the market. We ran and hid in the bush. The Bazingili was a huge, ugly man. Children ran away from him. But people in the village like the chief. Whenever there are disputes, he solves them with Wisdom. Nobody complains after the chief passed judgment. But he likes women. Oluma has many wives. Many of them are very young, just a few years older than me. I remember him taking one girl from our school to be his wife. She agreed because he is the chief. We laughed at her before. But she is happy. Being the chief's wife.

I told Mama that being the chief's wife must be fun. I asked her one day whether I can become one of his wives. Mama just laughed. She said the chief only chooses the best women in the village. Sometimes I dreamt that Mama was married to the chief. We played in the chief's compound. I told her the dreams, but she said it cannot come true. She is a widow and cannot marry a chief. I teased her about it and she just laughed. When Mama wants to make you stop talking about a subject she doesn't like, she just laughs. That is Mama.

This spot is my favorite. When I want to get away from the noise and talk of the village, I come here. I have the whole place to myself. No one seems to come here anymore. It is where I come to meet Mama. I come here to talk to her about my life. I wish she is with me every day.

Before the village became what today it is, a collection of shabby huts and rakubat, life was different. A lot was happening here. There were weekend dances. People gathered from the other villages around here for the dances. There was a lot of merry-making and laughter and life. I liked the dances. There was this young man from the neighboring village. He was tall and handsome. I admired his style and dancing moves. He was also an outstanding drummer. Everyone in the communities liked him. When he took to the drums, the rhythm was so beautiful that everyone joined the dancing. His manner was quite exhilarating. It was like the drum sticks were the extension of his hands.

All that is gone now. Nothing is left. You can see it in the faces of the people. They all look like zombies. It is just about surviving. Nothing more. How to get food for the children. How to scratch a living. I live in a crowded home. Extended family members fill the house. Also, it is not my real home.

I came to live with my auntie, Lena, after the death of Mama. She died at childbirth when she was giving birth to my little brother. Up till now, I do not know what happened. Or rather, I do not understand what happened. But my aunt said it was the baby that killed her. Koko is a big boy now. He can run and say some words. Auntie Lena is mama to him. Maybe when he grows up, I will have to tell him about

Mama. Our Mama. Auntie Lena looks after him. I cannot believe that he caused the death of Mama. He is so cute. I love to play with him and carry him around. He loves it so much. Especially when I take him on my back, and I am on all fours. He is my little brother. I promised Mama the other day I would look after him very well. She was happy about that.

Life is hard for everyone in the village. The war has caused a lot of suffering and destruction. It killed many young people. I know several boys who have gone to fight and never come back. People say they all died. The boys go to war; the girls stay at home. For the girls, life rotates around a routine that can be monotonous. Wake up in the morning; clean the compound; light fire. Put on hot water for my uncle. Go to the river to fetch water. Make porridge. Wash clothes that need washing. Cook food. Go back to the river. It is a cycle of work.

There is one part of this work which is fun too. To make the flour for our food, we have to pound and grind it ourselves. We use the big stone for this purpose. A friend once told me they use a machine in the town to grind flour. We do not have it here in the village. So, we do it with our hands, as groups. We talk and laugh and sing. It takes the strain out of the hard work.

There is no school anymore. The war has closed all schools. I love school. The teachers have all gone to fight also. The day our teacher left, he said he would come back. I hope he does. He was such a good teacher. He taught English. I love English. He made us read aloud in class and told us stories from big books. I missed school. I hope the war stops soon so that I can go back. From where I stand, I can see the long structure that is our school. There are only five classrooms in it. Those who finished school here are sent to the neighboring village to complete their learning. We were taught under the big Neem tree sometimes. We used to love it. Studying in the open.

The government now uses the schools as displaced centers for those who came to the village from other places. They are all in rags, hungry, and tired looking. There is little food to be given to them. Occasionally, some people come to the village with food. White people in big trucks with food sent from abroad come to see them. They provide them with flour and oil and beans. That is all. Because they need to buy other things, they sell some of their food to the village people for little money. To buy salt, for example.

I see them every day when I go to the river to fetch water. Their children play under our trees in the school compound. The women are always busy, trying to cook something for the children. The men have nothing to do. There is no work in the village anymore. They just sit around in groups, playing mongola, dug out on the ground near the market place. They play from morning to evening. They go home only in the late evening to eat whatever the women have prepared.

Mama stands beside me. I know she is there because I suddenly feel a cold breeze. I turn to her. She is smiling.

"I am happy to see you, Mama."

She holds me close to her, and we sit down on the bigger rock. She likes sitting in the same place every day. She also has her favorite spot. Like me.

"You are growing fast, my child. Soon you will be a big girl."

Mama's voice. She had the most beautiful voice. It had a slight pitch to it, which remained in your head long after she had gone. One cannot forget her voice. It has such distinctiveness. When I was much younger, she used to sing to us old songs from the past. She said the songs were sung during the harvest, as women cut the sorghum and maize. She had always led in the songs because of her voice.

"I have a lot to tell you today, Mama."

I stop to look at her. Where can I start? I have a lot of things to tell

Mama. She holds my hand and looks into my eyes. Her smile is very stunning. She is still so young. She has to go when she is still in her prime. I want her with me always.

Her smile reminds me of her picture, with Daddy, taken many years ago. It was black and white. Some kawajat took the picture. This picture sat on Mama's table in her room. It had turned yellowish with age, and because of many thumbing. She was kneeling near a big shrub and touching the tip of a leaf as if she wants to pluck it. She was smiling, happy to have her picture taken, and showing a set of teeth so white. She was the most beautiful Mama I had ever seen.

In the picture, Daddy was standing behind her, wearing white shirt and dark trousers. His face has a far-away look to it like he did not want his picture taken. Daddy did like a lot of things. Maybe that was why he left us so early. He disagreed with anybody. He even disagreed with the chief if he thought he was right. Daddy disappeared before Mama died. He was taken away by soldiers who came to the village. We have not heard anything about him since. Six years. Then Mama died.

"I am listening, Opiangwa," Mama says. "Tell me."

I want to tell her about Izaru, the boy in the village. He is trouble for me these days. Izaru is a good boy, but I do not like his ways. He used to be in the same class as me. But now he does nothing, like everyone else. The day I was coming from the river with a group of girls, all of us carrying water on our heads, he came from behind and tickled me. It surprised me so much that I dropped the whole bucket of water on the ground. It ruined the bucket. It was very difficult to explain to auntie Lena what happened. I was angry with him that day, although he seemed to like me. The girls thought so too. They teased me about him always since that day. Especially Kapuki. She is a naughty one. That girl. She talks about things we do not understand. Maybe because she is older than us, she knows a lot.

I know I am trapped. I cannot tell Mama now. Maybe later, some other time. When she calls me with that name, I know she is coercive. It is the name she knows means a lot to me. Opiangwa. I like the name. It has an authentic African ring to it. When Mama calls me using this name, I concede in anything. Not today, Mama, I plead inside.

"I have been a good girl, Mama."

"I know my daughter. I know you will make us proud one day. I hope the war ends soon, and you go back to school. Your father and I think highly of you."

"But life is hard, Mama, without you and Daddy. It is a struggle."

"I know you will succeed. Just concentrate on your goals in life. This situation will not last forever. It will come to an end. You have to be ready to move on with your life."

"Auntie Lena takes good care of us. Koko and me."

"Yes. Lena is a good sister. I know she will look after you like her own. Take care of Koko, Opiangwa."

Mama puts her arms around me again. Her caress soothes my heart. Emotion fills my inside, building up like a boiling pot about to explode. The moment took me many years back when I was just starting school. We were playing a game with the other kids in the school compound. I took my sandals off as we ran around, chasing each other in the game of sembelu, a form of tag game. I ran into a small bush behind the classrooms and injured my foot. There were broken glasses there that I had not seen. It bled very severely. I cried from the pain. The girls had to call the teacher who tied it with a piece of cloth and carried me home to Mama. Mama feared for me. She took me in her arms and calmed me down. I can feel that comfort now. The same feelings I had many years ago.

"I want all this to end, Mama. I want to go back to school. To study and be a teacher. I like to teach small children one day."

"It will — one day. I left you at the time you need me most, my dear. How I wish I am there with you every day."

Mama stands and looks around. Her face looks worried. She must be thinking a lot about us, our future without her and Daddy. There and then, I know what I will do to make her happy. I have to be strong, do my best in everything. I have to succeed in my studies when the schools open again. I have to accomplish that for Mama.

"Who are you talking to?" a voice says behind me.

It is auntie Lena. She stands there; her face scrawled in a stern and severe look. She is my favorite aunt. I love her, not because she is Mama's sister, but she is sweet in her own right.

I smile at her. She can be stern and severe when she has to. Like today. She must have been looking for me. I can sense the sharp talk that will follow, but I am not afraid today. I had spoken to Mama already. I can go home now.

I turn around, and Mama is gone. She has gone from where she came. Mama leaves as silently as she comes. I know she will be looking after me always from where she is. I know that because I feel her every day. I think of her in everything I do.

Auntie Lena stands behind me and holds my hand. I look at her. I feel sorry for her sometimes. Her sweetness is very contagious. You can never be angry with her. If only she has found a good husband to take care of her. She is always worried about us. Her husband spends a lot of his time drinking and cares less about the family. Auntie Lena is the backbone of the family now. She is a strong woman.

"I am talking to Mama," I say. I know she will not believe me. Mama died about five years now, and talking to her will seem bizarre. I do not mind that at all.

"You are day-dreaming again."

"No, auntie, I meet Mama here every week."

"If you continue to do that, you will not be able to take care of yourself in the future."

She does not believe me. Who will ever think that I see my mother? Can I even explain?

"But auntie . . ."

"Come here, my little one," auntie Lena cuts me short in her sweet motherly voice. "I know you missed your Mama so much. We are here for you."

My little one. Auntie likes to call me that. For auntie Lena, I will always remain so. I am still her little one, even if I am no longer that small. I want to tell her that I am a big girl now. Koko is the little one. But the sweetness with which she speaks makes it hard to contradict her.

"Thanks, auntie," I say. Thoughts of Mama again make me want to cry. Tears swell in my eyes and start to flow down my cheeks slowly. Before they turn into floods, I wipe them off with the back of my hand.

Auntie Lena comes over and holds me tied to her. She looks into my eyes, her sweet smile penetrating my heart and calming my inside with a fresh lease of affection.

"Come, my dear. Let us go home. There is a lot of work waiting for us at home."

Auntie Lena takes my hand, and we start going towards home. Going downhill is easy. The path is clear and hard. The early morning dew has evaporated with the first rays of the sun. Thick rain clouds, dark clouds rising from the east filled the sky. It is going to rain soon, I thought. The rain will be good this year.

I turn to look back at the place. Mama is back, waving to me. I am already looking forward to meeting Mama again.

3

Street People

H E WAS HURRYING HOME TO HIS FAMILY. THE NIGHT WAS STILL young, as they say, but you never knew how it would end.

Tunda walked out of the clinic, his mind in a haze from the tiresome work he had been doing since early morning. His small surgical practice in the middle of town had become very busy of late. The patients came from far and wide looking for him. He had made a name for himself without knowing it. And now that he was famous, he began to hate it.

He had seen all kinds of patients in his five years of medical practice in Khartoum. There were the curious and the psychotic; the silent and the talkative; the sick and the malingering. It was always a task to differentiate one from the other. The fear had been to make the wrong choices, and he had had his portion too.

And today was not an exception either. Tunda was still bothered by the last patient he saw, an older woman who had a rather vague complaint. He couldn't make head or tail of it. When all investigations are normal, convincing patients that there is nothing wrong with them is the hardest part. How do you tell an older woman that medicine had not yet found correct tools for diagnosis for all the ailments in the world?

For him, five years was not long enough yet. He just turned forty, and he has many years to learn and perfect his skills.

He walked to his brand-new white Toyota Camry. It gave him real pleasure every time he got into this car. It was very comfortable inside, and the air-conditioner soothed his aching body. And it flew like a dove. He placed his briefcase in the backseat and got in behind the wheel. As he drove away from the clinic, the time was getting way past eleven.

Tunda liked driving fast, but tonight was exceptional. He wanted to see his surroundings and feel the air. Today, he had the air-conditioner off and all the windows down, as he savoured the moments slowly. The street was empty except for few late-night travellers like him hurrying home.

And then he saw her, a lone figure under the bright street light, frantically urging him to stop. Tunda wanted to fly past her but thought for a moment. Maybe she missed her bus, a student hurrying to the hostel before the doors were closed or perhaps just a young female wanting help. He stopped the car.

The young lady walked up elegantly and looked into the car. She had the most beautiful face he had ever seen. As she came closer, he saw that she was of African origin, probably from the west of the country. Her high cheekbones gave her the looks of Marilyn Monroe, and she had the figure to go with it. The tight-fitting blouse she wore and an equally tight-fitting mini skirt accentuated her figure-of-eight shape. He took in all this in a second.

"Would you mind giving me a lift?" she asked. And she had the voice too, Tunda thought.

"Not at all. Get in please," Tunda replied, nodding his head too, unsure that she heard him.

She walked gracefully around the front of the car to the passenger side. The glare of the headlights illuminated her like theatre lights. Her place is on the catwalks, not the street corners, he thought. She opened the door and slid in. The car was suddenly overwhelmed with a strong perfume that could knock a new born baby unconscious. As he drove away, he looked at her from the corner of his eyes. Her silhouette against the streetlights enhanced the sharp facial features and curvy nose. She kept looking straight ahead. And she was just stunning.

"What do people call you, young lady," Tunda asked. It was just an attempt to break the heavy silence surrounding them. He hated small talk. It made him so vulnerable, unsure where the whole conversation would go.

"Pamela," she replied. "But my close friends call me Sunshine. You can call me that".

She giggled lightly, her soft voice filling the car.

An awkward silence fell between them as he tried to find the appropriate words to continue the conversation. He checked himself quickly as his mind went to his wife and children at home. It was no point salivating at every excellent work of nature he came across.

"And where are you going, my beauty," he asked, at last, his eyes looking straight ahead at the road. The crowded street was giving way slowly to light traffic as they drove further and further from the city center. They crossed the bridge as the goods train rattled past them in the opposite direction. The old metal bridge was shaking. This structure needs servicing, he thought, otherwise it may one day collapse.

"Home," she answered, in a laid-back attitude.

"Oh, fine. I mean, where exactly? I . . . ah, I mean, where should I drop you off?" Tunda stammered.

He was utterly angry with himself. It was not often that women had this effect on him. He cursed the moment he decided to pick her up.

She did not answer his question. It was like there was no need for an answer. Maybe it sounded stupid for her. He started small talk about the weather and the traffic just to keep his mind from her. She spoke in monosyllables in her soft dreamy voice. Oh heck, he thought, she must be mad.

"Am turning off here, lady," Tunda said as he applied the brakes, and the car slowed down. Since she had not given him any direction, he thought it best to drop her here. Tunda pulled up by the side of the road. He turned to her.

She just sat there, looking straight ahead and as if she hadn't heard him.

"I am not getting out. I am going with you," Pamela finally answered without looking at him a moment.

Tunda groaned. At first, he thought he didn't hear her well enough. She must be crazy.

"What do you mean? Look here, lady, or whatever they call you. I just gave you a lift. I thought I was helping you out. Now, what are you saying, ah? I am a married man with children. Where do I take you to in the middle of the night like this? Except to the police station? Maybe?"

As she made no move to get down, Tunda turned the car around and headed for the police station.

"I will scream; I will say you tried to rape me," Pamela said.

He stopped the car and looked at the girl. He was now confident she was a lunatic. What would he do if she did what she had threatened? Who would anyone believe his version of the story? Would anyone understand him?

He turned around slowly to face her and looked at her for a long time. There were lots of things that could go wrong. His very reputation was at stake. He could already read the headlines in the tabloids in the coming days: "Surgeon caught in the act," "Doctor in trouble," etc. His very career is doomed. He could not allow this to happen.

"Just what do you want, woman?" Tunda pleaded. His voice had lost its sternness. "Ask anything I can give, and I will give. You need money?"

His time was running out. Without waiting for an answer, he rummaged through his wallet and fetched several notes amounting to five thousand pounds, his night income at the clinic, and handed them over.

She quietly grabbed the notes from his hands as if she were afraid he could take them back and stashed them into her handbag. She got out of the car. Tunda gave a long sigh. He didn't wait to see her go.

He started the car and drove away, his mind swirling from the incident. He couldn't imagine what could have happened otherwise. His act of charity, of being a Good Samaritan in the night had almost cost him his career and family. How could he have explained everything? Could his family have accepted? What about the police? They are notorious for pouncing at such stories without verifying the facts. You are presumed guilty until you prove otherwise. He was glad it had not reached that stage.

But Tunda knew what he would never do again, day or night.

4

Escape

THE HALF-MOON WAS SINKING SLOWLY BEHIND THE DARK RAIN clouds. The dreamy shadows melted into the dark corners around the compound. In one corner of the compound, four tiny lights were shining. They moved. Black cats.

I stood at the door to my hut. The night was still early, but the town had already gone to sleep. There was no electricity, and the few diesel generators in the neighborhood had gone silent. It was tranquil. The children who had been singing in the compound next door had retreated to their homes. The night had come. I knew they would come for me one day. And when they do, I would be ready for them. "They" and "them" have no faces, but I had a fair idea who they were.

Juba 1992. It was a difficult time for the citizens of the besieged town. The civil war came to Juba for the first time. The rebels shelled the city several times. Citizens could hear the rumblings of heavy guns and fighting outside town. The army faced hundreds of casualties.

They lost hundreds more in battles. They had become jittery.

As if to revenge their defeat in the battlefields, they were bringing the terror into town. They were sure there were now many freedom fighters inside the city hiding among the civilians. They wanted to track them down, together with their sympathizers. It was a terrible situation in which the line between the guilty and the innocent became blurred. When they come for me, I would be ready. That was why I had become a light sleeper. I would wake up in the middle of the night and go out into the compound, moving around. I had the idea that when they finally come, they would find me ready.

Ever since my close friend told me that the faceless ones were after me, I knew it was a matter of time before they pounced. I fitted the profile of the wanted, although I had not done anything to warrant that. I was well educated, a professional in my field of teaching, and had become well known. For them, I was suspect. I saw how countless other people had been taken away in the middle of the night and never seen again. Families had been asking about the whereabouts of their loved ones, but there was no one to give them answers. When they take you to the infamous White House, the security detention place, it was the end of the story. Citizens incongruously named it. Everyone knew it was no luxury house. There was no "House," be it white or otherwise, just a series of transit containers both above and underground for keeping the detainees. Some succumbed to the midday heat and died from exhaustion. Few people had come out of the White House alive.

Suspected rebel sympathizers were randomly picked up from town and taken there and tortured for information. Due to the torture, individuals just came up with any names of friends so that they could be released. Many innocent men had disappeared. I didn't want to follow that path. I want to be different; I could be statistics. I knew of tens of people who had disappeared, picked up at night.

There had been instances in which decomposing bodies turned up on the River Nile. More often than not, the bodies bore signs of severe torture. Some of the dead bodies had wires and ropes around their hands and feet. Others turned up inside old Kenana Sugar factory sacks. You cannot recognize the victims due to the putrefaction. Everyone knew these were the works of the faceless ones. Fear held people in its grip so tightly; it had pumped out of people their last breaths and the willingness to live.

The night was as hushed as a haunted house. The usual barking of the dogs was not there. The typically slight breeze that swirled through the trees was conspicuously absent. The leaves were as stiff as rods. It was the perfect night for a raid, and I knew it. I was ready. I had a feeling that it might be tonight. No worries, though. I was alone and prepared. I had sent my wife and kids to stay with her parents. They would be safe there for the moment. I knew that the faceless ones would not spare anybody they found in their path that night. I prepared. I walked back inside.

Just two minutes later, I heard only two knocks. I opened the door. Johnny and Luambo slipped inside. Johnny was breathing like he had been running. His face broke into little sweats that glistened in the dim light coming from the kerosene lamp in the corner. I raised the flame to increase the brightness. He sat down on the stool by the door.

Luambo was a big man. He had the full chest of a boxer. He worked as a mechanic at the garage in the Hai Malakal area. He walked over and sat on the bed. It squeaked loudly as the strings took his heavy-weight. For a few minutes, nobody said a word. I knew they were not here for fun. It had surpassed us for a long time. There was no longer fun in a war game. That was what we were living — a war game.

Johnny and Luambo were old friends. We had grown together in the neighborhood and been to the same school. We had even dated the girls for some time. We had done all sorts of things together. Ever since we were young, we had been inseparable from friends. The three of us had gone through the highs and lows of the town. When we were at school and had to read Alexandre Duma's book, everyone started referring to us as the Three Musketeers: Athos, Pathos, and Aramis.

Outside it began to rain. It was not the usual heavy rainfall, with winds and thunder and lightning. It was just light rain, which could last for hours without end. The kind of rain that could fall all night. We loved this rain when we were young. We called it seke seke. It meant we could not go to school when it started in the morning. We remained at home, gathered around the fire in the kitchen hut waiting for hot porridge, seasoned with peanut butter. It was lovely.

"You have to leave tonight."

It was Luambo, Pathos, who broke the silence. He spoke in a subdued voice. The loud baritone voice had given way to a low-pitched tone that was way different from the one I knew.

"I am not going anywhere. It is my home, my town," I said.

"You can't stay anymore. When the faceless ones come for you, it will be the end. You can't fight them now. Not tonight."

"But why? We have prepared for this for a long time," I objected.

"No, you have not," Johnny cut in.

He was silent all along. He had been the quiet one of us three. He was the kind of person who let others speak first. He spoke only to put the final opinion and convince all — the wise one.

"They say a coward who runs away lives long to fight another day. You will have your time, Aramis."

Johnny liked the Three Musketeers thing. He was the one who gave me the Aramis name. We used to wonder why Aramis was not ending in "os" like the other two names. He had suggested they called me "Aramos." He was on the real name tonight. That was when he had serious issues to talk about with them.

I had figured myself standing to fight to the end. I had envisioned the final minutes of the fight. It was a suicidal end. Last man standing for the cause. But it was not to be. Not tonight.

"What happens next then," I queried.

"A man is waiting for you at the end of the path near the cemetery," Johnny said. His voice was shaky. Johnny was not a happy man tonight. He spoke with the voice of a man who had authority. He had made all the plans. I had no choice. "They will take you to the river bank where a boat is waiting to take you across. On the other side, you will be met by guides who will take you to the road to Uganda. After that, you will be on your own."

"You have to leave now," Luambo emphasized.

I knew I had no choice. I looked around the cramped hut. There was not much that I needed to take with me. I grabbed the small travel bag and stuffed two shirts and a pair of trousers. I did not have to change. I was wearing my jeans and T-shirts. I put on a large overcoat for the rain and stood up. All the while, Johnny and Luambo were silently observing me. I knew what was going on in their minds. We had spent a good part of our lives together. It was hard to be separated now.

"If they know I had gone, they will take you in," I said. I was making one last attempt to avoid going. "We have to go together."

"No, we can't, it will be sure proof that we were guilty," Luambo said. "You go. When it gets worse, we will leave. We will join you."

But how could they be so confident? I had known the faceless ones. They could be ruthless. The friend of a friend was to them as guilty as the friend just for being friends. Period. I was afraid for my friends.

Luambo walked to the door. He looked outside. It had stopped raining. The cold air from outside blew inside the hut. I tucked the coat around me more tightly.

"Time to go," Luambo said.

I took the rucksack and followed him outside. Johnny came up behind me and pulled the door closed. He left the lamp burning. It would burn until the kerosene ran out because nobody was coming back to the hut again.

We fell in a single file as we raced through the dark town pathways towards the cemetery. Luambo was keeping the pace, stopping from time to time to check the road ahead. When he stopped, we all knelt and waited for his signal to move on. We did not want to risk the chance of bumping into the security night patrols. They were as bad. Because of the six to-six-curfew, they charge anyone caught for illegal movement. Nightlife had died in town. The sporadic defaulters caught were drunks. In the morning, they were usually paraded at the police station and made to clean the police compound and toilets, fetch water from the River Nile. Their heads shaved clean.

Luambo led us through the furthest end of the graveyard, which was on the road that led to the river. The cemetery had no fences; it was bushy, with small paths that zigzagged between the graves. The graves themselves were arranged haphazardly. Many people had erected low barriers and big crosses around. In the dark of the night, they were like dancing figures. The occasional rats scrambled from our path and into the bush further away.

As we approached the river, a beam of light flashed twice from the direction of the mango trees. Luambo signalled again, and we dropped down, quietly. He waited. The light flashed once more.

"That is the signal," Luambo said. "Come, let us go."

I followed him, and Johnny fell behind me.

Three big men appeared as we approached. They shook our hands without saying a single word. He motioned me on. I stopped, hesitating for one moment. I turned around at my two friends. They just looked at me.

"We shall meet, brothers," I said, quietly. The silence was too much.

The only other sound that I came to hear was the slow movement of the water in the river, as it splashed against the river banks.

"Of course, we shall," Luambo interjected. "There is no going back now. You have to hurry."

I hugged each one and turned towards the canoe. One man already in the boat helped me on, and the others sat down at the tip. The man with the long stick started to paddle away from the banks.

From the canoe, I could barely see the silhouette of my two mates, as they disappeared into the darkness.

Half an hour later, I was across the river and further out from the town, on a small rising hill that, during the day, would have given me the beautiful view of the city. But not tonight. The darkness was complete, but I knew the general direction to my house from where I stood. Will I be able to see my family again? I wondered. A single gunshot broke the stark silence. A dog started barking. I turned my back and followed my guides into the darkness. The light rain started again. Despite my flight, I knew one thing, though: I shall be back.

5

Cousins

My MOTHER TELLS ME THERE IS GOING TO BE A FAMILY MEETING. I love family gatherings, not only because relatives converge in our house, or a variety of food is normally cooked, but also, particularly, because my cousins will be among the people coming.

Given that my father is the eldest son, our house is the natural place to hold the meetings. It has more or less become a tradition, something that we do every year—passed from generation to generation. That is what Mama tells me, but I am not sure how true that is. I guess she made it up so that it looks special. I did not think many families have these kinds of meetings.

Whenever I tell my friends in school that my cousins are coming because we are going to have a family meeting, they think it is weird. I forgive them because they do not understand the importance. For me, it is another opportunity to meet my cousins who live in Yei, a good hundred miles away from Juba, where I live. They drive to our house and stay with us for two days before they return. We catch up on each other's news, play together, and run around the house. We do things that all girls our age do. And we talked a lot.

The last time we had these meetings, it was much fun. The issues ranged from updates on family affairs to marriages. It also discussed the funeral arrangement for my grandfather. It was a big occasion last year. Father said it was a success because of proper planning and the family gatherings that bring ideas and sharing. He makes these gatherings something that we children always look forward to attending. Mother says the next family gathering will be next week, on Saturday. My cousins will come on Friday afternoon.

I have many cousins. My father has three brothers and two sisters. On my mothers' side, she also has a brother and two sisters. So, you can see how many cousins are going to come to our family meetings. When we were growing up, I used to find it hard to believe that all of us are related. We only know that we are very close because of regular visits. I came to know some of my cousins when we are quite older.

I have two older brothers, a younger sister and me. My elder brother has completed university and is working with a company in Juba. He is one smart man, my brother. My younger sister goes to the same school as me, although she is two years my junior. I will do my senior leaving exams next year and hope to go to university too. Two of my cousins are in the same class as me. The remarkable thing is that we are not only age mates, but also our birth dates are exactly the same. My parents used to throw birthday parties for us at our house. When my cousins come for the meetings, they all give a hand. The boys bring the chairs, put up the tents, and do many of the heavy chores. The girls are around the kitchen, helping my aunts with the cooking and going to the market. Since we were that many, we never hired anyone to help with the food. We did all our cooking and stuff.

Our house is not very big, but it is big enough for the gathering.

The children all sleep in one room, and the women occupy two rooms adjacent to each other. The men have to manage in the verandahs or outside in the compound. When the gathering takes place during the dry season, it is good because the rains will not disturb us much.

My father calls on everyone to take their seats. My uncles and aunts sit on the chairs arranged in a semi-circle. The seating arrangement ensures that they sit close to their wives and husbands. The young children will have to make do on the ground. The women lay mats out in front of the semi-circle, and we sat on them. However, my elder brother and cousins get seats with the adults. They have all made it to the family gathering. Earlier, they had food and drinks and just talked about many things except the meeting.

"It is good to see you all together again," my father begins. He has a loud voice. He can speak without a microphone, and many people far off can still hear his voice. He prides himself with that voice and distinguishes himself as a speaker of the family. Many years ago, I learned that my cousins call him the Bull behind his back. He knows nothing about the nickname. The gathering is one such occasion that he feels proud of hosting. "It has been a long time since we met like this. Our meeting today has many issues, which are very important indeed."

Mama has not informed us about the topic. She is very secretive about it, and we find it strange indeed. Previously, my mother would brag about what is going to happen in the meetings. When her younger sister was about to get married, she was very talkative about it. My mother was anxious about her sister. She was completely different from her like she came out of a different womb.

I remember when she visited us the last time. My mother talked to her a lot. She came to introduce her boyfriend. They talked for a long time that day. She had spoken highly about the gentleman. My mother knew his family and immediately approved. She gave her blessings, and the marriage took place. Mother had feared that her sister would fall for some of the young men whose sole aim was to spoil a girl and move on. That is how my mother described them: good-for-nothing men.

My sister is now here with her husband and their little daughter, a cute little thing that resembles My mother more than her mother. They call her Hadia, in Arabic, meaning a gift. She giggles and runs around the group now and then, with her hands outstretched, before returning to her parents. Her mother scoops her up every time and wipes the saliva dripping from her mouth with a napkin.

When the talks start, everyone falls silent as my father narrates the issues, and the uncles and aunts joined in the discussions and agreeing with many of the points. I notice that most of the problems are general: farms, housing, and school for the children. A few things about the family business in town also came up.

At that particular time, a beautiful young lady walks into the compound. She finds her way to an empty seat at one corner of the group and sits down. I lose track of the discussions immediately as I focus on the new arrival. She wears an African attire, a long flowing dress that sweeps the ground as she walks and has a large headgear as well. She is gorgeous. I have never seen her before in my life. All eyes settle on her briefly and return to the speaker. I see the women in the group are stealing glances at her, curious glances of those who want to discover her secret.

"There is something important that we are going to talk about now," my father says.

Everyone turns to the young lady sitting at the corner. My mind goes on a free fall of ideas as it tries to fathom the state of affairs. Is she the subject of the discussion? Why all the secrecy from the start?

"My son wants to marry," my father continues. "As you know, in our family, it is our tradition to introduce the bride to everyone."

There is a murmur of approval from all seated. The murmur is something between a "yeah" and an "aah." It suddenly dawns on me that my elder brother is, at last, going to marry. He had been reticent about it for some reason that I am yet to understand. He had confided in my father and planned to inform the family officially. The secret was coming out in bits. My brother just sits there, unmoved by the voices coming out and shouting congratulations to him. It is evident that the news surprises many in the family.

True, many are surprised. Alex is the quiet one. Among my brothers and cousins, he was the one that many did not believe would ever get married. Alex is timid, afraid to talk to girls, and minds his own business. When in the company of ladies, he speaks when spoken to and a man of few words. My cousins used to tease him that since he couldn't talk to ladies, they would have to elope with one for him.

"But we have a problem. When I spoke with my brother here, he says we need to talk about it as a family because of a certain reason."

My father turns to uncle Felix. My uncle likes to speak little. We always likened Alex to uncle Felix, that he has taken after him. The way things are moving, there could be something in the air. uncle Felix gets up from where he is sitting and goes to the front.

"I am happy to be here with you today," he began. There was no emotion in his voice, just the usual matter of fact voice, revealing nothing of the surprises to come.

One of my cousins crawls over to my side and whispers in my ears. "Nana, do you know that lady?"

I look at her. She is beaming, grinning from ear to ear, as if happy to have that lady among us.

"No, I don't."

"She is nice looking, isn't she?"

"Wait and see what happens, Tanya," I say and turn away from her. The other people are engrossed in what uncle Felix is saying.

"Come over here, Alex," he said.

My brother gets up from his place and moves to stand beside uncle Felix. He stands there, his face still in the fixed non-descript mode. He does not look at anyone straight in the eyes. He is focusing on a spot in front of his eyes that he alone can see, his face scrawls in a stare.

"My nephew here has brought up something that I had feared for a long time," he said. "I want to make things clear today. Some weeks ago, he brought a lady to see me, and he told me that she is his girlfriend, and they intend to marry."

He stops talking for a long time. I am sure something awful is going to go down. His eyes start to look funny, and his voice getting shaky. Everyone anticipates something is going to happen but did not know what. The family gathering is getting hyped.

"Before I got married to my wife, I had a relationship with another girl that resulted in pregnancy. However, she had to go away to another town, and I never heard from her again. I forgot about the incident and married my current wife."

He pauses again. I look at the faces of my uncles, aunts, and cousins. No one seems to know where this was leading. But I am not sure. I cannot tell whether they had prior information about the news unfolding or not. My father sits with his arms across his chest, looking straight at his brother. It is like he does not want to catch the eye of anybody. And what has it got to do with Alex, now standing there like a robot? He is as far away as he is near.

"As fate would have it, my nephew fell in love with my daughter, the cousin they have never seen and known. When they came to me, I knew immediately. She had been living under a different name. Her mother died; relatives raised her, gave her their name. That is why Alex never knew they are cousins until I told him."

He starts sobbing. His voice dies, and his chest starts heaving up and down like waves. He pulls a white handkerchief from his left breast pocket and wipes his eyes. It turns bloodshot with the few teardrops. He composes himself and looks around as if looking for sympathy from those gathered around him. My father starts fidgeting with his buttons and looks away towards the fence, where a group of birds had settled gracefully. Mama turns to speak to her sister in whispers.

"I have known all along where she is. I never told anyone about the incident. No one knew what happened. This story is what I want to tell you today. Also, I want to apologize to my daughter, for the years she stayed in the dark about her family. I want to welcome her back. For this reason, Alex can't marry her."

I smile. So, the beautiful lady sitting in the back is a cousin, after all. I muster some courage, stand up, and walk over to where she is seated. I extend my hands, and she takes it in a firm grip, all the while looking at me in the eyes.

"Welcome, cousin," I say, still smiling.

She gets up, and we hug. I take her hands and lead her to the front of the group. The two of us stand there, and suddenly everyone starts clapping and shouting.

Alex quietly went back to his seat. He walks like someone drenched by rain and with shoulder drooping. The weight of the revelation is too much for him to carry.

"There is something that I want to add," my father says as he stands up and walks to the front. The smile in his faces shows that the evening surprises are still not over. He stands there and takes his time before he speaks. It is like he wants us to go through some heartbreaking moments to figure out what is coming.

"The situation is not as grave as it looks, people," he finally says. "There are more than what is obvious here. I can assure you that all is not lost for Alex and Sheila here. When I heard of this, I made my inquiries and feels now it is the time to share it with all."

This meeting must be the most unusual family event I have ever attended. It is laden with one surprise after another. What does he mean by that statement? I wonder to myself.

"When I heard from my brother about the issue, I made my investigations. What I have discovered is very interesting, to say the least," he continues. "There are two things which are important here: the status of my brother and that of Sheila. First, let me start with uncle Felix as everyone calls him. I have found out that he is not my real brother."

A long sigh goes through the people gathered as my father utters these words. Everyone turns to his or her neighbor in complete disbelief and amazement.

"That is not true," someone says from the back.

"What evidence do you have against uncle Felix," another says.

I am shock. I turn to my cousin Tanya. She, too, is in a state of utter disbelief. Her face is dull and lackluster. Her expression ranges between a stunning shock and sad depression.

"Hear me out, please," my father urges. "I am not telling lies, and Felix knows about that. The elders brought him to stay with my family when he was a baby after his mother died. My father cared for him. His birth parents and close relatives are never known, and that is why he found a home with us. Because he is not a true blood brother, his children are not related to us. However, because he stayed in our household, he becomes a brother to me. But since there is no blood relationship, my son can still marry his daughter."

My father pauses to look around the gathering. He sees the happy faces, the gloomy faces, and the not-so-much-concern faces too.

"We will slaughter a goat to break the relationship," my father continues.

My brother is speechless. He gets up from the seat and sits back again. He turns around to look at me, sitting right behind him. His mouth hangs open like a panting dog. Then his face breaks into a smile as he catches the eyes of his bride-to-be.

6

Independence Day

July 7, 2011. 10:10 am

JOHNNY DID NOT EXPECT A WELCOMING PARTY ON ARRIVAL. HE did not envision a large party of little girls dancing to drum beats, shaking their waists and heads in unison, dressed in cowhides and beads and ostrich feathers. Or a long line of men and women smartly dressed, waiting to shake his hands one after another. He only saw these on television when African presidents or dignitaries visited other countries. It was for celebrities. Not for him.

He was returning home to the land he fled several years ago and did not care less about a reception party at the airport. In fact, he did not mention it to many friends that he was coming home for the independence celebration two days away. Only one person knew.

The weather was humid and hot. It had rained a few hours earlier,

Johnny could tell. This being July, the dark rain clouds were still hanging from the sky like runaway kites. The sun peeked from behind them, like a mischievous child playing hide and seek with an unwilling father. A slight wind was blowing as he walked away from the plane.

Like the other parts of the airport, it has not changed much. The pale grey structure had not seen any facelift in the past two decades, let alone a layer of fresh paint. This airport was destined to be a new hub in Sudan back then, connecting the Southern part with East Africa. The French construction company known by the acronym CCI left the structure half-finished because of the civil war. The only thing they completed was the runway running parallel to the old one and the new control tower.

A building was going up alongside the old terminal, a new terminal he heard about? At least they should have worked hard to ensure it is ready for the great day, Johnny thought.

There were flags everywhere. A large banner on the side said: "Welcome to the 193rd Country in the world". The cut-out letters that spelled Juba still stood where it had been all these years, next to the Juba International Airport sign, on top of the terminal building with the three pyramid-shaped roofs.

There were no luxuries of conveyor belts, metal detector gates, etcetera–things that were ubiquitous of airports worldwide. Maybe change had not yet come here. The airport had the feel of a remote outpost deep in the Sahara Desert or Siberia. Alienated.

Being a light traveler, Johnny had no luggage. He walked to the immigration desk, presented his passport. He felt a slight awkwardness, coming home as a foreigner carrying a foreign passport. He was not alone, though. He could see several other South Sudanese who were with him on the plane had passports from other countries too. The conflict had displaced thousands of people like him to seek resettlement in faraway places. South Sudanese were scattered like the Jews to the far corners of the world. There were South Sudanese Canadians, South Sudanese Americans, South Sudanese Australians, and South Sudanese British. If there were South Sudanese Chinese or even Japanese, he had not met them yet. Nonetheless, many were now returning home like me for the Independence Day celebrations.

A young man approached him and offered a taxi. He politely declined, telling him that he had a car coming to pick him. Then he saw him. The man is holding a small white placard with his name written in black on it. Johnny walked over to him and introduced himself.

"Karibu nyumbani," he said. Welcome home.

The man speaking in Kiswahili must be a Ugandan. His accent and complexion said he was from somewhere in central Uganda. He knew that very well because he lived in Uganda for many years before he managed to get resettled. Uganda was his second home. This brought him memories of many years back when some of his friends had to flee Juba on foot, to find refuge across the border.

"Asante sana," he replied. Thank you.

Johnny had lived in Uganda for a good part of seven years. He left the camp in Adjumani in Northern Uganda and went to stay with his uncle in Kampala. His uncle worked in the liberated areas of South Sudan; his family remained in Kampala. Johnny attended secondary school and went on to a teacher's training institute in Moyo. However, after completing, he found that teaching was not for him and started the process that led to him being resettled far away.

"Jada asked me to pick you up. Do you have other luggage, sir?" he asked.

"No, that is all I have," Johnny answered.

"By the way, my name is Jogo. The car is this way. Can I have your bag?"

"It is okay. I will handle it. Thanks Jogo."

Johnny followed Jogo across the small drive and into the parking area. Jogo was driving a battered grey Toyota Crown. By the look of it, it had seen better days. The color had disappeared in some places where panel beatings were done. It definitely needed a makeover and some paints.

The parking area was bustling with many other brand-new cars, though. A good number of the vehicles belonged to non-governmental organizations, with the names of the organizations branded on them.

Then there were the many boda boda motorcycles milling around.

He hated these things in Uganda. They were nuisances, accident-prone, with many casualties. He had hoped the country did not adopt this kind of transportation, but it looked like it was already too late. They arrived with a big bang.

Jogo opened the boot. Johnny stashed his small bag and got in beside the driver. He realized he was on the wrong side of the vehicle.

"Have we changed the way the vehicles are driven in Juba," he asked. "I did not hear or read that in the news."

'Why?" Jogo asked.

"The driver is on the wrong side, like East Africa, like in Uganda."

"Bwana, many of these cars are brought from Uganda, that is why."

Very funny, he thought.

If the outside of the car was awful, the inside was even more. The scarlet seat cushions had turned a fading color somewhere between that if a rusted iron and a fried banana. They were torn, as if an angry cat was let loose inside the car, ripping the padding apart. The greyish dashboard was dull and unimpressive.

As he started the car, music filled the inside. He could tell the song was in Luganda too. It was like the only thing working correctly in the car was the stereo system. The car rolled out of the airport parking onto the main road. Johnny reminisced his days in Juba and felt a heaviness in his heart as the buildings flew by.

He put his head back and absorbed it all.

July 7, 2011. 04:25 PM

Johnny sat under the cool shade of the mango trees at his hotel. The prefab buildings were tiny and were too damped for his liking. However, he had slept for five straight hours. The flight was long, and he needed some rest.

They dropped him off and told him Jada will come for him later. After his rest, he had a shower and came out to the restaurant to have something to eat. Johnny chose a table closer to the river, with a good view of the water. Out in the river, he could see a lone fisherman in dugout canoe floating down with the water flow.

Johnny used to come to this very place many years ago. He used to come here to eat mangoes and swim in the river. Sometimes they came here fishing. Now, the whole riverside had been turned into hotels made of tiny shipping containers.

Jada came in with two other men when Johnny was wrapping his meal. He had a fried chicken with chips and soup that tasted like soapy water. He had gone for the familiar, not wanting to disturb his stomach yet with unknown foods. It seemed he missed on the soup, though.

He stood up, and they embraced.

"Good to see you, man, he said. His voice had not changed much from the time they spoke on the phone. How was your flight?"

"Thanks. Good to see you too. It was long. Very long," Johnny said.

"Ah, I know. I traveled that route too. That is why I said you had to rest before we could meet. Welcome to Juba."

Jada sat down, and his two friends moved a chair from the adjacent table and sat around.

Johnny could see that Jada had become a huge man. He was skinny and lanky many years ago when they were together in Juba during the early war years. They used to tease him. His nickname was the mosquito. He was told to walk around with stones in his pockets to give him some weight, or otherwise, the gust of wind would sweep him away. He mentioned it to him.

"I am no mosquito anymore," he said, laughing. His voice was hoarse, with a background gruffness to it. "I am a bulldozer now, mate."

He gave a prolonged hearty laughter that shook his whole body like an earthquake, his big flabby belly moving up and down like waves in the high seas.

When we sat down, Jada produced three mobile phones from his pocket and put them on the table in front of him. It must be the latest trend in town, walking around with several mobile phones for the different networks in the country. When he left the country many years ago, the only telephones were the landline, which barely worked in many places. Government offices and some elected officials had the luxury of phones.

One of the phones rang. Jada picked the sleek new phone on the table. He excused himself and walked some distance from the group to speak. A long telephone conversation followed.

Johnny chatted with the other two men who he never knew. He found out that they work together in a logistic company ferrying goods from East Africa to South Sudan. There is an insatiable need in the new country for everything from cement and building materials to food such as grains, sugar, and flour. Their company imports these items in bulk and sells them on to local retailers from their big warehouse in near Jebel Kujur. Occasionally, they also supplied non-governmental organizations.

"That is big business, my friend," Jada said when he finished the conversation. He pulled his chair back and sat down slowly. "I just got confirmation of a contract to supply the army with sugar for all their garrisons in the country worth more than twenty million dollars."

"This is big," Johnny said. "You must have lots of connection all the way to the top brass."

Jada lit a cigarette from a pack he left on the table and blew the smoke as small balls in the air. Johnny did not remember when Jada started smoking.

"We now run the show in this country," he said.

"How comes?" Jada asked.

"Things have changed. Yes, things have changed. When we kicked the Arabs out, we now hold the business. You see, these jallabas used to cheat us out of our own money. Now we are in control. All you have to do is make sure you know the right people; have the right connections, and you are good."

The place was getting livelier as the night wore on. The live band on the stage started an old, slow Congolese number that brought reminiscence of the ancient times in Equatoria Inn when Johnny and friends used to rush dance to Lomerika Jazz Band music every Saturday and Sunday evenings.

A group of white expatriates joined a large table not far from them. They looked like aid workers. A couple got up and started dancing to the music, holding each other tightly. They moved slowly with the music, encouraged by the soft tunes and the cool breeze coming from the Nile and wheezing through the mango trees.

July 7, 2011. 11:39 PM

Johnny retired to his room after the long day. His hot water was not functioning when he wanted to take a shower. The front desk informed him that the heater is broken, and they will have to bring him hot water in a bucket.

When it came, he showered. After many years outside the country, he had not used a bucket for bathing. Ferrying water with his two open palms and pouring on his head just did not work for him anymore. He got a small cup from the dressing table and used it. He immediately went to bed and fall into a deep sleep.

July 8, 2011. 09:01 AM

Jada had sent a car to pick Johnny up from the hotel. It was much different from the rundown one that brought him from the airport. He had left the best for later. The car was a brand-new white Toyota SUV, the one he later learned popularly known as a V8. It was the best vehicle for the bad roads. It also had luxury written all over it.

The driver took him on tour to see the changes that had happened to his city after many years.

They drove from the hotel towards Konyo Konyo market, which was bustling with activity. He saw several groups of people sweeping the roads profusely. It was an army of people with brooms and shovels and wheel burrows working in the early morning heat.

They crossed the Malakia market and went towards Mahata Yei, which had changed entirely. A new building has started to erupt in the once empty space that used to serve as a bus stop to Yei town.

At the University roundabout, Johnny asked the driver to take him John Garang Mausoleum, where the former Vice President of the Sudan and President of the Government of South Sudan was buried. Johnny had previously seen the place on TV numerous times. They drove towards Customs. The Customs roundabout was full of people. The site that used to be a residential area and military barracks by the mausoleum has been converted into the Independence Square in which the ceremony would take place. Military police in their ubiquitous red berets sealed off the area to pedestrians and vehicles. They were directing people away from entering the grounds. The flags from different nations could be seen lined up along the road.

"There is no access today. The people are preparing for tomorrow," the driver said.

Many soldiers in different uniforms sat under trees and the big shad resting. They were participating in a mock parade preparing for tomorrow. Several onlookers were also waiting.

They drove around some more. Johnny sat there, absorbing the changes that had happened to the town since he was last here.

July 8, 2011. 01:15 PM

They met for lunch at the restaurant in downtown Juba near the Ivory Bank building. It was crowded.

"Food has become big business, bro," Jada said. He was responding to a question from Johnny. And that Juba did not have so many, and people used to eat at home.

"You see, with the peace, official government work starts from 8:30 Am to 5:30 pm. There is a one-hour gap for lunch. That is why the food business has flourished."

"There are not many empty spaces in Juba anymore," Jada said, as he cleared his plate of rice and meatballs. "Even the spaces we used to play football is gone."

"They call it development," Jada said.

"Really?"

"That is a story for next time. If you are done, I want to take you to meet some friends."

"Where are we going in this new country if we don't have playgrounds anymore?" Johnny persisted.

"Ah-ha, you started to see now, eh? It is a different country."

July 8, 2011. 11:59 PM

The independence celebrations had already started late that evening. The crowds had gathered in the streets and partied.

At the hotel, Johnny sat with friends who came along with Jada to usher in the new nation. The tables were full. There were as many white people in the sitting area as were the South Sudanese parties. The secluded place adjacent to the stage had been booked by a politician for a private party. A large dinner table was set up there for him and his guests of pretty ladies in skimpy dresses.

As the clock struck midnight, the crowds cheered, the band played a song, and fireworks were lit. Then the gunshots started.

As far back as he could remember, Juba had always had problems with guns during celebrations. Growing up in the city, Johnny knew that celebratory gun shooting at night had become part of the game. You hear gunshots on Christmas Eve and New Year's Eve. He remembered people firing their guns during an eclipse of the moon, too, a tradition that used to involve banging on pots and plates and barrels. It had been replaced by firing guns.

The government had warned against shooting of guns in the air. It seemed to have fallen on deaf ears. The shootings went on for several minutes and died down as suddenly as they started.

When Jada and his friends left, Johnny stayed up for a little longer, listening to the jazz band playing old Congolese songs that transported him in time.

July 9, 2011. 11:04 AM

Johnny woke up with a headache and found that his hands were strapped to the bed. He could faintly hear voices in his room that he could not recognize them.

He opened his eyes slowly. The headache became worse. He tried to raise his head to look at the people in the room, but he could not. His whole body felt like he had been run over by a garbage truck. He went back to sleep.

July 9, 2011. 03:45 PM

The voices were deafening when he woke up again. He felt slightly better and opened his eyes.

He could tell immediately that he was not in his hotel room. The mattress was softer; the curtains were light blue. And the room was freezing. A TV mounted on the wall opposite his bed was showing the independence celebrations at the John Garang Mausoleum. South Sudan TV panned between the jubilant crowds and the podium where a speaker stood. It then dawned on him that he did not go to the square.

"So, you are awake," Jada said, as he entered the room. He had a worried look on his face.

"Where am I? What happened?" Johnny asked.

"You are in a hospital."

"Why? What happened?"

"I came to pick you up so that we go to the Mausoleum for the celebrations. When you did not pick my call, I had to come to your room. We could hear the phone ringing, but you were not picking. The hotel broke the door, and we found you are unconscious and unresponsive. We had to rush you to the hospital. Who were you with after we left last night?"

Johnny could vaguely remember that when he stayed behind for some time, a lady came and offered him a free drink – she said it was a compliment of the hotel management – for the Independence Day. When he was going to his room, he became dizzy, and the same lady offered to take him to his place.

"You have been robbed," Jada said. "They took everything from your room. Everything, except for the old mobile phone you carry. It must be their parting gift."

His headache returned as he tried to analyze the situation. On the TV screen, the crowds were ululating and shouting as speaker after speaker took to the podium. The Speaker of the National Assembly read the Declaration of Independence; the Sudanese flag was lowered, and the South Sudan flag raised. The crowd roared. Hundreds of tiny little flags waved in unison.

The nurse walked into the room and said she wanted to give him another injection. He turned his head and looked at the wall. He became drowsy again when the band started to play the national anthem for the very first time officially.

"Oh God bless South Sudan" are the last words he heard as sleep took over again.

7

The Teacher

"WE ARE GOING TO BEAT UP OUR MATHS TEACHER," POPE SAYS. The three of us are sitting together in our den after the last day of school: Pope, Friday, and myself. When Pope speaks, we all listen. He is the leader. He is a bit taller than the two of us but has a small build and no muscles to boast of. However, he can climb trees faster than a monkey and can chase a chicken until it becomes fatigued enough to be easily caught. Despite the heat, Pope likes to wear his sweatshirt over his faded denim and leather shoes with a pointed tip.

In contrast, Friday is short and stout like an athlete, which he is not. He has a round baby face; his eyes are set close together, with too much hair covering most of his scalp. When I first met him, I found it funny that he is named the days of the week. He just laughs and says his brother is called Monday. If his mother had not died early, they would probably have completed the days of the week in their family. I want to tell him that I have never heard of a person name Tuesday or Thursday but decide not to.

"Do we have to do it?" I ask.

"Are you afraid?" Pope asks.

"He will identify us."

"He will not."

"What is the point then? Beat up a teacher who will not know who did it and why?" I say. "Don't you think it is better if he knows that we beat him up for a reason so that he does not repeat it when the new term starts?"

He makes it sound like an everyday activity. The three of us are in the same school in the same class taught by the teacher. We have been together since we joined the school six years back and are now poised to move on to senior school in a year. I am part of the gang now, yes. I wear our T-shirt, yes. I chant the songs we learned in our hideout, yes. But beating up a teacher, ah, ah, not me. I do not think so. I do not believe and cannot do so.

"I don't think it is a good idea," I say.

Pope ignores me. He wipes his right hand on the hard floor, removing small stones and dried grass, leaving a cleared area on the floor. The building we are in is at the edge of the old cemetery at Hai Malakal. Pope and I discovered the half-completed house some time back. It has three big rooms that we now use for our own things. However, the high green roof is in place, which shelters us from sun and rain. Because the doors have not been fixed yet, goats and dogs and chicken wander inside when we are not around. Their droppings are all over the place, and we have to clean it every time. I find human excreta sometimes, long hard ones, and flat ones like the person who deposited it had diarrhea. We have to deaden the smell by pouring sand on them.

On the cleared area on the floor, Pope carefully lays out the war arsenal. The weapons of choice are simple: red pepper powder, a catapult, and a club. Pope tells us he borrowed the red pepper from the women in Konyo Konyo market. The women have stalls where they lay out their wares. The red pepper powder is in small plastic bags, laid on the stall together with little bags of tea, salt, sugar, and several types of foodstuffs. Friday, and I know what Pope meant when he says he borrowed. When he steals things, he says he is just borrowing them and will return. He never does, of course. The same for the red pepper powder now.

Pope says we are not to harm him much, just a small beating to teach him a lesson. He likes that. Barnabas teaches us class lessons, and we teach him a lesson in the street. A beating he shouldn't die from is, therefore, in place. Beating him up will surely make Pope feel happy, satisfied.

"None of us is big enough to confront the teacher on his own," I say. 'I still think that we have to find another way of doing this thing.'

"I believe we had discussed that before," Friday says.

I know Friday is a fighter. He fights big boys, small boys, and anyone who crosses his path. The big boys never bully Friday in school because when he starts fighting back, it never ends in the school. He will follow you with it back to your neighborhood. He will wait for his chance when you are least expectant of him, will pounce with whatever weapon he has. He will keep fighting you until you call for a truce. He never does that himself. One day in class, one of the big boys laughed at him after he failed a straightforward test. Friday fought him in the class. They were both suspended for one week from school and had to cut grass in the playing field.

Pope cracks jokes when he is in a good mood and shuts up when he is unhappy or with no money to call his own. That is Pope. He also serves as an altar boy at the neighborhood church and has done so for a long time. He participates in high mass with the bishop and carries the bishop's hat for him. In fact, that is how his name came about. He claims the bishop cannot hold mass without him. I do not believe him. But that is Pope being himself.

When you see him on the altar, he is so quiet, so tame. His white flowing gown and the red collar vestments transforms him into a saint. He moves gracefully during the processions, his hands he clasps in front like in prayer, with calculated steps in unison with the song or the tune from the church organ.

After a high mass, we meet late at night in our den, and Pope brings altar wine and communion with him. I do not know whether he steals them from the church or during the time it is being prepared. He says it is no sin since it is not yet blessed. That is him, always with the right answers. For the wine, he says they are extra bottles. One cannot argue with him. If you try, you are definitely on the losing side.

"We must teach him a lesson," Pope finally talks. He has been too quiet. 'He is a big-headed teacher, brutal and will kill someone one day with his beatings. Do you want that?"

"I don't want that," I say.

He looks at me like I am an outcast, with no arms or legs, and one eye in the middle of the head. His eyes, though, are wide open like he has been smoking weed. He does smoke weed sometimes. We all do. I do not like it much. The last time I tried, I coughed the whole night, and my father almost found out. Pope's eyes are bloodshot. Maybe he has smoked one roll already, maybe two. Or even three.

I know why he is determined to do that to the teacher.

Pope is angry that his girlfriend, Yolanda, was humiliated and caned in the class by the math teacher. To be truthful, she is not his girlfriend. Not yet. I am not sure whether Pope will win Yolanda's heart. He has competitors, for sure. And she is rich, has wealthy parents. She is dropped to school in a car and picked up at the end of the day. Never mind that it is a Land Rover 110. While we miserable lot have to walk the six kilometers home, come rain or shine. Pope has no chances of winning.

She was tutored at home, wears a clean uniform to school every day, while my dear friend scrapes along with one that has to be washed if at all every other day. When he plays football, that means the shirt has to be cleaned. By the middle of the first term, it is already fading from over-washing, with no replacement in sight. How can he claim her as his? She has a change of underwear every day, new, clean ones. I know because once she fell while playing in the school field and her skirt was blown over her head, and we all saw the brand-new clean rose-colored underwear without blemish.

Math's teachers come in all shapes and sizes and are the most vicious creatures in the school. Teacher Barnabas is one of them. The teachers come to school prepared to massacre pupils. When they arrived in the morning, they will send the school prefects, who are usually older boys, to go cut sticks for them. They do not like canes from the neem tree, which gets broken with just a few strikes. The favorite stick, which is resistant to breaking, is from a tamarind tree. This tree has sour tasting fruits that can be made into a drink by soaking them in water. We used to suck on the nuts, like sweets, after removing them from the pods – they leave your tongue and inside of your mouth raw and sore. That is the tamarind fruit.

Yolanda was caned for not answering a question. Teacher Barnabas is going to pay for that. When we met at the club that evening, Pope was fuming. I believe that is when he hatched the plan to chastise the teacher. Maybe, he wants to bring Teacher Barnabas' head on a silver platter as a trophy for Yolanda to accept him. Our religious education teacher once told us a similar story from the Bible.

Pope says the plan is simple, and we can execute it without him knowing who did it. For me, that is important because not only is he my teacher, he is also a family friend. Teacher Barnabas visits our home sometimes, and my father always asks him about my performance in class. They were buddies at Rumbek Secondary School a long time ago.

He looks much older than my father, though. He must be at least ten years his senior. He tries to look like a young man, dyeing his greying and thinning hair black every week, tacking his shirt above the protruding round belly. He resembles a clown I once saw in a magazine. I wanted to ask my father why he is so merciless and beats pupils that much. But I did not. I was afraid my father will tell him, and he will cane me in class again. I still remember the last time he did that.

Pope hands the red pepper to me, and I carefully place it in my pocket. He carried the club, and Friday has the catapult with several small and rounded stones he picked from the gravel mount near the den. We file out of our hideout and head for the joint where the Teacher Barnabas goes every day after school to drink. Pope tells us that the place is usually crowded with customers from midday to late at night. There are many customers, and they sit in small groups to swallow their orders. They are served by little girls who bring bottles and small glasses to the customers. Although they have tables, the bottles are typically hidden under the tables, away from prying eyes. Pope knows all that, and he tells us.

Pope is in front, then Friday and, I follow several reasonable steps behind the leader. He walks very fast, his school bag dangling from his back. He leads us through some narrow passages in the compactly clustered neighborhood of thatched huts and random fences made of papyrus and reeds and rusted corrugated iron sheets. There are no toilets in this place, I can tell. We pass through passages filled with the pungent odor of urine and booze and feces. Friday turns to look at me, his hands tightly holding his nose. He speaks with his eyes. I motion him to continue, pretending I can handle the smell. He stumbles across a fallen bamboo pole and almost hits his head against the mud walls of a hut.

We get into a clearing just across the main road. Pope stops and points to a house a few meters away from us. It looks like any of the homes and compounds around. I can see just two huts in the

SACRIFICE & OTHER SHORT STORIES

compound, with several shelters. The fence is too low, and I can see
the people inside, in groups. Their voices start to filter to us like the
white smoke rising into the sky from each of the other surrounding
compounds.

Pope motions again, and we move to the side of the building closest
to us.

"We wait here," Pope says. "I will move to the further side. Friday,
you take the lead."

I take my position and squat. I wait and wait some more. No one
seems willing to leave Mama Nyoka's just yet. Mama Nyoka makes
the deadliest brew in the area. Her followers also come for the suku
suku, the highly toxic one made from fermented dates. I know all this
because Pope tells us. The drink is not like the wine Pope sometimes
brings to us from the church. No. It is a much, much stronger drink.
I tried it once I did not like it one bit. I decided to stick with stolen
altar wine for now.

A man walks out of the house and stands near the papyrus fence. He
unzipped his trousers, his hands shaking, and urinated loudly against
the fence. From my vantage point, I can hear it hitting the ground like
gushing water from a broken hose.

Then I see him. Teacher Barnabas walks out of the house. His attire
wholly changed and waggles from side to side. He is bubbling some
incoherent words as he walks. His once smart tucked in shirt is now
out, with the shirt half-buttoned from up. His hair is now unruly
and shabby. A small boy runs out of the next compound and makes
fun of him, as he flaps his arms to chase him away. The boy leans on
the electricity pole laughing, his right foot on the pole, and his arms
akimbo. He wears a yellow T-shirt that has become dirty. His equally
dirty pants have no bottom, replaced by two big gaping holes that look
like oversized rimless spectacles. I saw that when he turned and knelt
down to pick a stone.

I wait for a signal from Pope, who is several steps behind me now at the next street corner. Our plan rests on what I had to do before Pope and Friday rush him in. I felt in my right pocket for the lump. It is still there. The sun has gone down, but it is not yet dark. It is suitable for us so that he does not recognize us easily.

The teacher stands his ground in the middle of the road as if undecided on which direction to go. The small boy is still watching him from a distance. He calls out names, but teacher is not paying attention to him. He moves two steps forward and three steps backward. One time he almost falls but steadies himself with a herculean effort and remains standing. He sways from side to side like a eucalyptus tree during a thunderstorm.

Pope signals that I move to disable teacher. My heart is beating fast, very fast, and I cannot breathe normally anymore. Small sweat forms on my back and face, like I have been doing some heavy work. Will I do it? Will I be able to come behind him, even in his intoxicated state, tap him on the back, and when he turns, pour the red pepper in his face? Will I be able to then call out to Pope and Friday to hit him with the club and punch him repeatedly? Will I be able to stamp on his head and knock out his front teeth as a permanent testimony of our actions? These thoughts race through my mind as I make short steps towards teacher, who is now swaying on the road. I turn to look in Pope's direction. He is waving me on, but I can barely see him clearly. Friday is nowhere to be seen. I take another step.

Out of my right side, I hear a loud sound coming closer and closer to where I stand. I turn to look in the direction of the sound. Before I can figure out that it is a vehicle, it is almost on top of me. I jump back from its path. When I turn back to teacher, I see him flying high in the air, his arms flailing about as his body turns. I hear a thud seconds later as he hit the ground and rolls up into a mass of torn pieces of flesh and clothes and mud. Before I can close my gaping mouth, the car speeds off even faster down the road and disappear. The small boy yells and runs back into the house from which he came, calling on someone's name. I see blood gushing out of a cut on his forehead, forming a small pool on the hard gravel road.

On the first day of the new school term, the headmaster called the three of us to the front of the assembled pupils and teachers. He thanked and praised us for saving the life of Teacher Barnabas. The headmaster said if it was not for our quick actions and responses and being courageous, he would have died a terrible death. Teacher Barnabas stepped out from where he was standing with the other teachers. He had a sling made of white bandages across his neck, holding his broken left arm. A long scar across his forehead from where the blood flowed that day distorted his features. He smiled as he shook Pope's hands, then Friday's and then mine. I noticed that his two front teeth were missing.

8

Runaway

THE BUS STATION AT THE OLD CUSTOMS MARKET WAS STILL AS QUIET as a cemetery early in the morning. The last glittering silver stars in the sky were waving goodbyes and signing off. The women selling tea at the shacks close by were already out in force. Dust rose in the air as they swept the ground around where they were going to sit. The tables were placed conveniently near the corner of the shack, atop which were numerous empty milk cans stuck three high. Other plastic and glass containers nestled and fought for space on the already crowded tabletop. These containers contained tea leaves and other exotic ingredients for making sweet-tasting and highly scented tea.

I pulled a stool from the many stuck together near the tree and sat down. The lady closest to me eyed me with the eye of an eagle, curiously. I had been walking very fast for the past thirty minutes from home. I felt tired, and my breathing was up. My feet hurt badly. In the darkness earlier on, I hurt myself as I climbed over the fence. I wanted no one to know.

The previous night, I had placed two old chairs against the wall, away from view behind the bougainvillea in the compound. The thorns from the bougainvillea caught my dress and almost tore it from my body. As I struggled to free myself while up on the wall, I lost my balance and fell. I landed on one knee, which hit the ground hard. It hurt badly.

My only worldly possession was a bag where I had stuffed my three changes of clothes, a pair of sandals, and a small photo album. The little money I had was tied in a small cloth around my waist. I had nothing much. I never had new clothes for the last two years. My neighbor's daughter had been generous enough to give me her old clothes.

The woman finished with her cleaning and brought out two charcoal stoves. She poured charcoal from a plastic bag on the two stoves and shook them. She then stuffed old newspapers under the stoves and lit the fire. At first, it did not light, as the match stick broke in half. She threw it away and pulled another one from the matchbox. After wiping her hands on her skirt, she struck the match again. This time it lit, making a hissing sound like a snake. Slowly, she brought the lighted match to the newspapers, which caught fire immediately. She took another paper, tore it in half, folded and twisted it to make it long. She then picked the fire from one stove and lit the other.

After this ritual of lighting the fire, the woman put the stoves some distance from her and adjusted them to the early morning wind to fan it. White smoke rose from the stoves, curling, and dancing in the wind as it rose higher and higher.

By the time the charcoal had caught fire, the daybreak was approaching fast. More people appeared in the vicinity. Being the weekend, there were not many people in the street. A man walked passed in a hurry as if he was on the run. He almost tripped himself on a small branch that had fallen from the tall, shady neem tree nearby. He cursed under his breath and hurried on.

When I turned back to the woman, she had already pulled the stoves. She was a heavy-set woman. The stool was too small for her, disappearing under her huge buttocks. Her kitenge wrapper unfurled as she sat down, exposing her large thighs. She pulled them up again and stuck the piece around her waist.

She filled two large copper kettles with water from the yellow plastic jerry can and put them on the charcoal fire, which was ragging hot, fanned by the wind. I watched all her movements. She did her job with the devotion of a worker, knowing precisely what she wanted to do. It reminded me of my mother. I did not want to think about my mother now; otherwise, I would not accomplish what I wanted to do. I pushed the thought from my mind and concentrated on the lady in front of me.

All the while, she had not said a word. Maybe, she thought I was a lost girl or worse, a street girl who just crawled out of the bush nearby to disturb her.

A man came and pulled a chair.

"A cup of tea, please," he said.

"Tea is not yet ready," the woman spoke. At last, I heard her voice. It was a soft mother voice, just the right pitch. You will have to wait a bit.

"No problem," the man said. "I am in no hurry. It is still early in Africa anyway."

The man was dressed in oversized blue overalls. He looked like a mechanic. His overalls were dirty with black spots on them. Back home, the driver had an overall similar to that. He wore it every time he worked on the car. He wiped his hands on his clothes every time they get dirty and sticky. That was the color on the man's overall. I had always wondered why mechanics like to keep their overalls dirty.

The man in blue overalls took out a cigarette from his breast pocket and lit it. He took a long drag until the cigarette tip was getting red. He then puffed the smoke out slowly. His features looked familiar to me as he smoked.

I turned back to the woman. She had removed one of the pots from the stove and replaced it with a deep-frying pan. She then added oil from a small plastic can. Near her, she had a cooking pot, where she had made dough. She took a small piece of dough, rolled it with her fingers and dropped it into the oil. It sizzled loudly, as oily froths appear in the frying pan. I knew she was making legemat, the tiny doughnut-like puff balls people liked to have with their tea in the mornings. She repeated these steps until the frying pan was full of the sizzling little pieces. They turned into rounded shapes of different sizes. She used a perforated ladle to turn them around until they were entirely brown. She removed the balls one by one into a plastic container. When she removed all of them from the hot oil, she repeated the procedure.

The pot on the stove started making noise as it boiled. The lady turned around, took a small aluminum plate from the table, and laid it carefully near her. She got one of the little teacups, put two small spoons full of sugar. After that, she put a small tea strainer over the cup and added tea leaves from a tin. Then, she got the pot with boiling water and poured the water into the tea leaves to make a cup of tea. After removing the strainer, she stirred the tea slowly, without making any noise. Satisfied, she raised the plate and looked at me.

"Pass it to him, please," she said, looking at me straight in the eyes. "My little girl is not yet here to help me."

I looked around. There was no other person within a hearing distance. For one moment, I thought she was talking to someone else. Slowly, I put down my bag, which I was carrying on my lap all this time, and got up. I reached over the milk cans on her table and grabbed the plate. I took it over to the man. He held the cup without looking at me.

"Give me some of the legemat, too," he said. "For two pounds."

The woman counted two pounds worth of legemat, put them in another plate, and handed over to me again. I took it to him. Since there was no table in sight, I put the red Coca Cola crate upside down and place the plate of round balls on it, in front of the man. He then looked up at me.

"Is that you Juana," he said, surprised. "What are you doing here early in the morning? Are you all right?"

Now I knew why he was vaguely familiar. It was Banja, the mechanic who used to repair the vehicle in our house. He had grown a beard, which hid his face. He was a friend I never wanted to meet at this hour. My plan was about to be ruined.

"I am fine, Banja," I said hesitantly. I did not know what more to say. I could not answer the second part of his question. How could I tell him I was running away from a place I had come to call home for the last two years? How could I tell him all that I was running away from? "I am traveling to Yei town. For a holiday," I lied.

I was already afraid that word would get back before I had traveled far. I was determined to be as far away as I possibly could. I turned around quickly, picked up my bag, and ran towards the buses in the distance. The time is not yet up for the coaches to move, but I had no choice. I walked and found my bus on the far side of the station. Bags and luggage were being loaded on top of the bus. I rummaged through my bag and pulled out the ticket. I walked to the bus and got in. Banja had followed me to the park, but it was clear he couldn't locate me. He lingered around from bus to bus. The bus was still empty as he came to the door and peered inside. I sank deeper into my seat and kept my head low. I could not afford to go back to that home, I just could not. He backed away and left.

It was like an eternity before the rest of the passengers started climbing and taking their seats. A woman with two kids came over and sat in the seat next to mine. She pushed her bag under the seat in front of her. One of the kids climbed on the seat and tried to peer outside through the window close to me. I took his tiny hands and held him steady as he gazed through the window, smiling happily.

As the bus pulled out of the station, the heaviness in my heart lifted little by little. The further the bus traveled on the bumpy and dusty road to Yei, the lighter my burden became, as I left the terror of my past behind to face an uncertain future.

9

Casualty

IN THE ENCLOSURE NEXT DOOR TO WHERE NYAMBURA SLEPT, THE single cock crowed at the usual time. The cold early morning breeze blew through the tiny window in the circular mud and thatched-roofed hut. The sun rose in the east, between the mango tree and the tall twin pawpaw trees. That night, the usual gunshot was also heard, breaking the eerie silence of the night with a deafening, heart-wrenching echo, reminding everyone of the dangers that abound every night.

Right behind the hut he shared with his brother, Nyambura had a small patch of land that he used for planting. His father was adamant that he learned the art of farming the land. How else could a man live if not from farming? For his father, the education he was giving his son had been forced on him when he was a boy. He gave in just because the other children in the village were going to school. In his heart, he knew it would not bring much change, for his children must dig the land and live off of it. He had seen countless children go through the school but who never got anywhere, only to come back to the village and start all over again with farming. He wanted to give his children both options. That was why Nyambura had a small farm for planting tomatoes and beans.

At just eight years old, he had been doing fine with his little farming experience. Ever since his father gave him the piece of land to try out his skills, he had loved the practice. His tomatoes had grown bigger and bigger every day and had started to produce small flowers. The beans had crawled all over the place. They had begun eating the green leaves already. He would have to put some posts in between the plants so that the creepers could climb without covering much space. The tomatoes plants would need small supporting structures, too, when they started developing berries. He would have to go to the forest and collect some wood to make the necessary structures. Maybe, he would become a great farmer one day, his father told him.

Or maybe a cattle herder? Nyambura never liked going after the cattle. His father had taken him several times to the cattle camp, but he never liked it there at all. Sleeping beside the smelly animals under the moonlight, covered in ashes to ward of the mosquitoes was no fun for him.

The old rusty gong brought Nyambura back from his dream. The whole school shouted as one, the roar coming out of hundreds of tiny mouths crying out in unison. The kids ran out of the classrooms into the main playground in the middle of the school. The school was not that big, six classrooms and teachers' offices in the shape of a poorly drawn 'U.' Being the beginning of the year, their uniforms were still bright and new, the green shirts, khaki shorts and skirts shining in the midday sun. As they ran out, the small bags with thin straps dangled on their backs, the same on every kid. The bag had a UNICEF logo emblazoned and were filled with books.

The long war had come and gone, and now children must go to school, the chief had said. The elusive peace had at last been found. Nyambura had no memory of the war. During the war, they were moving from one camp to another as refugees with his family. He was too small to remember anything. He was probably too small to remember the night their village was attacked and destroyed to the ground by the high-flying planes sent from Khartoum. He could not have known how his family had to run through the bush as fire rained from the sky. Maybe, he would understand when he grew up. His mother had told him the stories, but he could not comprehend them well enough. Perhaps, one day he would. Nyambura thought about his father. He never knew his father. His mother had told him that his father died the day he was born several years ago. He still could not come to grapple with this reality. Maybe the stories were not true. He had believed deep inside that one day, he would return.

Nyambura stopped at the far end of the school compound to await the rest of the team. Ever since the schools opened and classes resumed, they had been exploring the areas around the village like crazy. Just the four of them brought together by friendship: Jada, just turning twelve; Wani, eleven; Bidal, ten, and Nyambura. They had been inseparable right from the start of the school year.

Jada headed the group. He has a big physique for his age and commanded respect among his peers. Jada seemed to know everything and had answers to all questions. When he did not know something, he always said, I will find out. He always did. The teachers liked him, too.

When the whole group had assembled, Jada led them off the track towards the forest path. They stopped under a mango tree behind the school and took off their school shirts to reveal football jerseys underneath. Since it was Friday and there would be no school the next day, they stashed the sweaters into their school bags. The day was for exploration. The boys always planned something different every day of the week. Last week they had gone towards the other side of the river on a dugout canoe to the mango fields where Jada has his uncle's plantation. Although the season was still early for mangoes, they had gotten the half-ripen ones and ate them like a salad with salt, pepper and lemon, until their mouths became sore. During their expeditions, they always returned home late in the evening in time for the evening meal.

Jada led them through the shrubs and bushes as they filed behind him. He was making quick struts, his school bag dangling on his back with every step. Soon they were sweating in the afternoon heat, even as they trudged through the forest path with the sun appearing now and then through the trees.

They came out into a clearing on the far side of the village. Women were working in the field, using their small hoes to clear weed from the groundnuts field. These fields had been no-go areas just six months before. When the conflict ended, several people were maimed by landmines and other unexploded bombs there. People said the village was at the frontline of the war and was heavily mined. Now the fields were safe for cultivation.

Several groups had worked in the fields to clear it of those mines. It was painstaking work to watch. Before their schools opened, the boys used to climb the trees near the village to watch the men work. They wore strange-looking contraptions and stooped low to the ground, with their machines whining in the heat of the day. From time to time, they would stop, and one would kneel down to plant red-triangular flags in the spot. Another team will follow to dig it out. The road from the village was once dotted with these red flags. The road had a fading sign, which said, 'Stay on the road always: landmines around!' Although the roads are now free of landmines, no one had bothered to remove the old sign.

One of the women working in the field raised her head and looked in their direction as they filed past, not wanting to be identified.

"Hey, Jada," the woman shouted. "Where are you going?"

Jada ignored her and continued on. His troops, including Nyambura, followed behind carefully.

"Am talking to you, young man," she persisted. "Are you up to some mischief?"

Jada realized he could not shake her off by merely ignoring her comments and questions. He stopped and turned towards her. She just looked at them, her eyes asking the same problem again.

"We are taking a walk through the fields, auntie," he answered.

"Don't get into trouble out there," she warned. "Or I will tell your mother."

Without another word, the group scuttled off, beaming smiles across their faces as they moved further away from the women in the field.

Several minutes later, Jada stopped at a hill, and the others stood behind him as he scanned the scene in front of him. He stood there like a commander of an army, surveying the ground where he would lead his troops into battle. He remembered coming through here with his father some months back and seeing some old trucks in the bush. His father told him they were old military trucks, remnants of the war days. He wanted to explore them today with his team.

He saw the landmark he was looking for, a tall coconut tree, way to the side. He bounced down the hill towards the trees and crossed into the bush. He leveled the tall elephant grass with his feet as he waded through it towards the tree. The others followed without a word.

Then he saw them. The trucks were covered in overgrowth, hidden from view by the overhanging trees and shrubs. He forced his way through the thick bush on to the side of the first vehicle. The three green trucks were in a straight line like they had deliberately parked that way a long time ago.

"Here they are, folks," Jada shouted; the excitement was palpable in his unusually shrill voice. "Let's see what we have got here."

He crawled through the canopy of the first vehicle in the line. It looked intact, aside from the rusty body parts, the shredded rat-eaten seats, and the layer of fine dust that had settled on every part of the interior. Jada climbed into the truck and sat at the wheels. He tried to turn the steering wheel, but it got stuck.

The other boys climbed in the back. Nyambura went around the vehicle and jumped from the end. The truck had been carrying some things, by the look of the items there. Wrappings and old, dirty clothes filled the back. Several wooden boxes lay broken, covered with cobwebs with grass growing out of their sides. There were probably snakes out there too, Nyambura thought. He immediately climbed down and followed Jada to the second vehicle.

Nothing was exciting around the two other trucks, except for the last one, which was completely burnt out. The tires were gone, only the iron rims remained. The body parts made of wood were all gone, as well as the seat cushions and other plastic components. Jada climbed again into the driver's seat; he sat on the iron springs, which were rusty and smelly. In one corner of the cabin, a nest sat, covered in feathers. It looked like a bird had made its home there.

Jada got down from behind the wheel and looked around the vehicle.

"I saw these trucks many months ago," he said. "I never knew what they were until now. Army trucks."

"Why are they here?" Nyambura asked.

"These were here from the days of the war. These were enemy vehicles. They carried their soldiers."

"What happened to them? Why is nobody towing them away to use?"

"Probably damaged beyond repair," Jada answered.

They walked around the vehicle to explore the rest when Nyambura's feet got caught up in something.

"What is this?" he exclaimed.

Jada stopped and picked a small rotting bag. It must have been lying there for ages from the look of it. As he pulled it from the ground, a round metal object dropped into the grass.

"What is it?" Nyambura asked.

"Looks like iron balls. There are two of them."

"Iron balls?"

Jada had not seen anything like these before. "We'll take them with us," he added.

Nyambura took one of the balls in his hand. It was surprisingly heavy for its size. It appeared like an orange. While checking it, he saw that the parts were rusty with age. He slipped his ball into his pocket.

"Let's go back. It's getting late", Jada said.

Later that night, Nyambura took out his iron ball and looked at it carefully under the kerosene lamp hanging from the roof. He was alone in the hut; his sibling having gone out to the compound. Although it looked like a ball, there was a funny protrusion on one side, and the surface was rough. He examined it, wondering how to use it. Maybe it was not a ball, he thought. He shook it and placed it closer to his ear. No sound could be heard. There was nothing inside he could hear. He found a protruding metal sticking from one side of the ball and pulled it.

The explosion was heard a mile away, shattering the peace and silence of the night.

10
—

The Dream

S HE CAME TO ME AGAIN LAST NIGHT. IN A DREAM. I WAS SITTING outside the hut under the mango tree on a warm afternoon. It was late October. The mango season was still two months ahead but the trees had already hundreds of little green mangoes adding their weights on the sagging branches. It was the dream I was having for the last several nights. The same dream. Lulu was sitting on a stool, her favorite stool curved out of a tree trunk by the carpenter who lived by the river Nile and who specialized in these kinds of crafts. She wore the long dress made of African fabric that her uncle Lokulenge brought her from Congo, the one with the colors of green and orange and red and blue making up a kaleidoscope of vibrant art work. She had the same material wrapped tightly on her head, with the knot to the front. Lulu was saying something but I couldn't hear it. Her lips were moving, mouthing the words one by one. Nothing came out. Maybe she was not saying anything, just miming to herself? She stood up and raised her right arm, pointing towards me. I could see that she was very thin. Aged too. Then her body transformed. Her ears grew long and her flat nose grew and extended and curved down to touch her thick upper lips. Her eyes shone like a bright torch that hurt my eyes. I woke up. The sun was shining directly into my eyes through a gap in the window curtains. The beam picked up the minute dust particles swirling in the room, stirred by the heavy ceiling fan.

Later that day, I walked into the kitchen through the back door at the restaurant where I work. It was on the corner of W Ponce de Leon Avenue and Clairmont Road in downtown Decatur in Atlanta. The chef was busy at work, with the team of assistants and helping hands. The kitchen was hot. I could never get used to the heat of the kitchen. Never. It felt like one is deep inside a gold mine shaft or an underground bunker. (Yes, a bunker like the one I had escaped into many years ago. The memory of that bunker will forever be engraved in my mind) The big steaming pots on the rows of gas cookers on one side of the kitchen wall produced vapor in the room. Sweat mixed with the smell of food and veggies.

I yelled a "Hello chef Ricci" to the chef but he did not respond. Chef Giuliani Lorenzo Ricci was a great cook of world renown capabilities. His mind was probably in the day's menu he was working on to feed his increasing number of insatiable customers from all over the city who frequented this restaurant. Ricci came from a family of chefs since his great, great grandfathers back in Italy. His family had served in the kitchens of great Italian monarchs for generations. His was a specialty kitchen – serving only exotic foods – mainly sea foods of all types. I came from a landlocked country and never really seen any sea food before or the sea for that matter. The thing out of the water of the Nile River I had eaten was a tilapia or the Nile perch. In this country, I had come to know what people ate from the seas. Creatures that I saw in books only many years ago. The live crustaceans crawled about in the three huge water tanks in one corner; lobsters and shrimps and crabs and snails and shell fishes were all there. I never would have imagined myself eating any of these things. I have seen people thronged through the restaurant doors to devour and enjoy these beings.

The staff at the restaurant were like mini united nations. The cleaners, the servers, the dish washers and the cashiers were from all over the world. I had to compete with the likes of the Mexicans Diego Ramirez D'Souza, the new man who joined us at the restaurant just a month back, the West Africans like Mamadou Cisse from Senegal and Ife Ikechukwu Obi from Nigeria and the Indian Amitap Krishnan. And of course, there was the little man from Burma. Maybe the chef liked to have a multi-cultural staff in this melting pot restaurant. Those of us that have worked at the restaurant for a long-time time affectionately called him Dada. He is a father figure for all. His calm demeanor and soft voice imparted around him an aura of a religious leader than a sous-chef. If cooking were a religion, Ricci would be the high priest.

Before I started my afternoon shift at the restaurant, I took my lunch out to the parking lot and sat on the stone benches. I unwrapped the package and placed it on the stone table beside the bottled water I got from the fridge in the restaurant. My lunch was two slices of tuna sandwiches with shredded lettuce and tomatoes. I always brought my lunch from home with me every day. It was cheaper that way. Although the restaurant allows us some foods some days, it was out of bounds to eat of the restaurant foods. I couldn't eat sea food every day for the rest of my life in this country. So, I brought my own. Someday I had pasta with mincemeat and tomato sauce. Other days I had left over foods from the night before. It had always been cheaper to bring your own food to work instead of buying from the restaurants in the down town area. When I got my pay check, I always treat myself to some good pizzas and real African food from the *Habesha* Ethiopian restaurant down the road. It reminded me of home. It reminded me of my mother. And Lulu.

I know Lulu was trying to tell me something in the dream. The way she was looking at me, pointing, she wanted to say something. I know it. But what it is I could not understand. And why the same dream every night though?

The Ethiopian restaurant reminded me of my mother's cooking from many years ago. She loved cooking. My mother did. She could make a meal out of anything in the house. She had a small kitchen garden behind the huts in our compound with all sorts of veggies growing in there during the rainy season. When it was rainy and she couldn't go to the market to get whatever she had in mind for food that day, she would just cover herself and ran into the rain to pick from her garden and make a meal. A meal of green peas leaves with hot ugali goes down very well when it was cold and wet outside. As children, we loved that.

Diego Ramirez D'Souza waddled over to where I sat. He placed his lunch box on the stone table and sat down. He was a fat man. His belly sinks in front of him as he walks, and waddles like a duck. And short, probably just five feet three inches. He was going bald from the center as his hair thinned out. He wore a white shirt, with rolled up sleeves exposing tow giant tattoos of a dragon spiting fire on his left and right upper arms. He wore khaki trousers and an old, black Nike jogging shoes that had probably seen better days. The laces were of different colors: the laces on the left foot was black and on the right dark brown. The red Nike sign on the left shoe was starting to peel off.

"This is what I eat ever since I came to this country," he said. He looked at his meal before he took a bite and looked up at me. The mayonnaise from his sandwich slipped down the left side of his mouth. He looked like the big fat man on a TV commercial for a Big Mac. He wiped it slowly with the back of his right hand. He belched loudly.

"Why don't you change what you eat every day, try something different," I said. I figured he was looking for a conversation and exaggerating about his food. Diego lived alone and has not gotten around to marrying just yet. He is waiting for the right time, he said once. He liked to talked about his coming to America, as he called it. His vision of discovering the American dream and making it big.

"Are you a Lost Boy?" Diego asked.

"Why do you want to know?"

"I heard they came from Sudan. Are you not from Sudan?"

His reference to the refugees who were re-settled from Sudan during the conflict and became popularly known as the "Lost Boys of Sudan" intrigued me. The boys and girls were as young as 6 or 7, who fled Sudan on foot to Ethiopia and later some got to Kakuma refugee camp in Kenya. Thousands were later resettled in America and their stories popularized in books and films. Some made it into celebrity status and others wasted in the streets of America searching for the American dream. I am not surprised even Diego heard the stories.

"I am from Sudan, but I am not lost."

He laughed.

"I mean is that not the way you are all called here in America?"

Diego couldn't understand how I got here. To him every Sudanese in America is a lost boy. My story is different from the others, though slightly. It was not in the papers anywhere. Not in the papers he tried to read any way. How I came to work with him in a semi-dark kitchen washing room, cleaning dishes and carrying garbage in a restaurant far away from the land I was born in. Maybe I should tell him how I fled from the Sudan fifteen years ago, fleeing from the high altitude Antonov planes that rained fire from the sky over my village and how I hid in a bunker dug by my father when I was just ten years old. The Antonov, flying high in the clear evening sky, made that monotonous droning sound that reeked of death and destruction.

I should tell him about the several bombs that landed near us that day and that when the plane finally left, that I had to quickly run. Would Diego understand that mother was separated from us as we headed into the bushes with hundreds of other families and their children? We never returned home. I never did. We walked through the bushes for days, avoiding the main roads and heading in the general direction of Uganda. *As long as we keep the River Nile to our right side, we are in heading to Uganda, the elderly man reminded us always.* We survived on the Nile water and some of the little fruits we gathered along the way, traveling for two gruesome weeks. We harvested crops from deserted villages along the way and uprooted cassava. Some people died; young children died of hunger and starvation and exhaustion along the way. Only a small group of us made it to the refugee camp in Koboko in Uganda. Tired, hungry and worn-out. I stayed with my uncle in the camp for three years before the UNHCR resettled me and some other young boys to the US. I first came to Minneapolis, Minnesota, before I later moved to Atlanta, Georgia.

That was fifteen years ago when I was separated from my mother. I was hoping I could make enough money to bring her here. To be with me and live the dream life she would have wanted. And they would come with Lulu, too. My Lulu.

Lulu was trying to say something to me in the dream. Was she waving? Was her hand raised up? My mind started losing the details of the dream. There are few people who could interpret dreams and Diego is not one of them. I could not tell him my dream, this one or any other.

Lulu is the love of my life and I am going to marry her and bring her to America. We met through my cousin back home on the phone. She was introduced to me several years back and I had been planning to make enough money to complete the traditional marriage so that she could join me.

But here I am working as a dish washer at a restaurant I could not even afford to eat in. Diego Ramirez D'Souza had no idea.

"I am not lost, Diego," I said.

He laughed again. Lightly.

I laughed too. Although it seemed funny to him, it was not to me. I know why I laughed. I could still picture what he told me sometimes ago. Diego had told me his story time and time again. He may not be lost himself but he had a similar passage to this country called the United States of America, albeit in a straight kind of way. Maybe to him, everything is laughable. He wanted to laugh his way through life. Laughed his way through work. Laughed his way through the difficulties in America and make millions.

Diego loved to tell his tale of how he crossed the Mexican border at night, with the help of smugglers and hiked through the Arizona desert, avoiding guards and dogs and the occasional local vigilantes who wanted to keep them out at all costs. He managed to elude them all and lived in Tucson for a long time before he moved due East and ended up in Georgia still searching for the elusive American dream.

"Why are you here with me then?" he persisted.

"I am searching for what you are searching too," I said.

"In a restaurant?"

"Where do you want me to start? Hollywood?"

Diego pulled out his lottery ticket and waved it in my face.

"*Esta es la salida, Amigo,*" he said. "This is the way out."

When Diego is excited about something, his round face with sleepy eyes shines like a full moon. He becomes animated and engaged in this state that you will think he could go into a trance. His limited English will always fail him and he turns to Spanish to express himself, oblivious to the fact that the people around him may or may not understand him. The lottery excites him that much.

"Are you still dreaming of winning the lottery?"

"This is the way out of this place you called work. Do you think you will succeed in this country by working in a restaurant washing dishes? Man, you got to think big. Have a plan to pulled yourself out of this to live a decent life."

Diego was serious. He had been doing this for the last several years. He told me. Every day, he would go to the grocery shop at the corner of the W Ponce de Leon and buy the two tickets for two dollars. He did it so religiously for the last several years without missing a day. Every weekend when the draws for the week were published and his numbers did not win anything, he kept promising himself. Next time, Diego. Next time.

"What will you do with all that money, Diego? You will go nuts." I teased him.

His face beamed and he chuckled. He looked like someone who had already won.

"I have big plans for the money."

"Good luck," I said. "Remember me in your kingdom when you become a millionaire."

Living in a new country, away from home was not easy. Everyone knew that the odds were stuck against them. There are stories of immigrants who succeeded in the country. It had always been said that America is the country of immigrants. That immigrants built the country. That if you work hard you could become anything you wanted to be in this country. Land of opportunities. Everyone could make it here. All these are true, but only a handful can figure out how. Diego thought he could by winning the lottery one day.

My journey in this country so far has not been fruitful, to say the least. When I first landed my first job was working in a cold and damp place cutting up chicken, freezing and packing chicken while I attend community college. This job was so tiring, I spent half my days sleeping and had little time to study. I had to postponed my exams several times. I thought investing in education was the only way out of poverty in this country. I moved out of the chicken cutting place to other odd jobs here and there around Atlanta. I worked in stores selling cloths in JC Penny, Macy's, Kohl's, and H&M. These stores offered minimum pay jobs paid per hour. Nothing seemed to keep me down in these places. To make things worse, I always came under the supervision of harsh and mean supervisors who were there just to frustrate the hell out of me. I was picked out of scores of other for odd duties and humiliating things. I thought my life was jinxed.

After finishing my community college, I still couldn't get a good job to sustain me properly. I went to work for McDonald's at their outlet in downtown Atlanta. Although management was great and I worked hard, I still found myself unable to break out of the circle of poverty. I had to compete with other immigrants like me from all over the place. We were all vying for the best deal out of the work place. Everyone wants to be in the good books of the boss and have a shot at promotion and maybe get into the management line. Maybe one can become an assistant supervisor, then a supervisor and maybe a manager one day. All these ambitions caused problems between us. Back-biting and reporting to management what we said in private conversations hurt these prospects. Management used informers to keep taps on staff.

I finished my lunch and went inside the restaurant leaving Diego behind. He would sit there for another hour before he made it home after the shift.

The call came when I was just finishing up tiding the kitchen and getting the warm dishes out of the dish washer. The assistant chef told me my mobile phone was ringing. I left it on the ledge closer to the cashier to charge. He brought it to me where I was.

It was Kaku. I didn't expect a call from her, not at this time even.

The fact that she called at this moment raised a red flag immediately in my mind and my heart missed two beats. Then three. It was the same feeling I had when I heard that my father passed away. I had not seen him since the day I left the refugee camp in Koboko fifteen years ago. I had only been in this country for two years when I received the call that fateful day.

The fact that it was Kaku calling me added to the mystery. She had never been calling me for a long time. The calls from people you never expected were usually bad news. I immediately thought of my mother.

"Is mother ok?" I asked.

The telephone line was not very good. I heard my voice talking back to me as the echo travelled across the Atlantic to Africa and back.

"Your mother is ok, Bojoi. It is Lulu. She is gone."

"Who? When?"

"She died in a car accident"

My heart sank low into my stomach and hot sweat broke out on my body. I could not hear what she was trying to say even when I asked the question myself. I hang up. Could bring myself to ask too many questions. How did it happen? When did it happened? Who was with her? I would call back again sometime later and ask those questions.

As I walked out of the kitchen, the staff could see that I am not ok. They tried to ask but I just raised my hand and kept them at bay. I do not think I could explain much further this. I need time for it to sink in. I need the time to digest the fact that I would not be able to see Lulu again.

The dream must have been a warning that something bad was about to happened. I wish I had called her when the dreams started coming. I would have listened to her voice one more time. One last time. Lulu came last night to say good bye to me. She was waving bye, bye!

I went back to parking lot and to the stone bench. Diego was still sitting there. He was engrossed on something in playing on his smart

95

phone. He turned the phone upside down when I sat down in front of him on the bench. When he does that, he is certainly watching porn. I did have the stamina to ask him. what he was watching. A group of small boys were playing football. The real football that Americans called soccer. In a country crazy about American football, it is odd to see young teens playing the beautiful game. Somethings changed in front of our own eyes. A black bird settled on one of the branches of an evergreen tree nearby and slowly started to sing a dull monotonous tune that sounded like a dirge.

I spend the next few days locked up in my room. It fells claustrophobic and suffocating, but I didn't get out. Chef Ricci said I could stay home as long as I needed. Life seems to have come to an end abruptly. Like a serene movie with a sad ending. Maybe Diego Ramirez D'Souza is right about one thing: that I am lost in this country searching for the American dream. Maybe it is time to go back home to Africa. La salida, as Diego would have said.

II
—

Romancing the Bloom

I MET LELISHA IN THE CENTRAL HALL OF UNION STATION. SHE WAS bubbly as usual, her smile revealing a perfect set of teeth, white as milk. Lelisha had her signature dress, multicolored African *Kitenge* fabric that reached just above her knees. She had tight matching head scarf lightly, leaving a large part of the thick dreadlocks uncovered.

I took her left hand as we stepped out of the station building. I felt the warmth of her soft palms, electric pulses shooting up my arms. I remembered the first time I felt this. Exhilarating. I met Lelisha at the for the first time at a school fair in DC six months earlier. She came to the event with a friend, who I had known for some time. I immediately connected with everything about her: smiles, laughter, personality.

It took us fifteen minutes to walk down Louisiana Avenue NW to the United States Botanic Gardens on the grounds of the US Capitol building. The August sun was shining brightly, few clouds hung in the sky, and the weather was forecast to be very hot. It turned out to be right in the early 90s.

By the time we reached the gardens, we had sweated under our clothes. Lelisha's sleeveless dress stuck to her bare back as she shifted the black leather handbag strung over her shoulders from one side to the other. My bald head felt like I had water splashed on it, and my brain was cooking inside.

The queue had formed and gone around the building. A sign pointed us to where it started. We followed the sign, round the building, then a corner towards the back of the block. The line of excited men, women, and some children seemed endless. The people looked relaxed, moving one or two steps and standing still, talking. Each group engaged in their own animated talks like they had the whole time in the world in front of them.

I was distraught. Lelisha was thoughtful.

"I think we should just forget about seeing the plant," I said.

"I came all the away to see it," she said. "No going back now."

She kept moving forward. I followed.

We moved further down the queue, which did not seem to have an end. More and more people followed us patiently as we walked along the sidewalk, clogged by human figures either going to join the back of the queue or, for those who had already seen the plant, going away towards the Metrobus stop down the road.

The impressive building, with its iconic steel and glass canopy, resembled the Crystal Palace in London. I could see the trees growing inside from where he stood, the tall palm trees reaching to touch the glass ceiling like they were trying to escape a lunar mission station.

All around the building, there were plants of different types. What amazed me more was that each of the plants, big or small, had its name written on it in a small placard. It resembled the name tag of a valet in a hotel. The labels had both the botanical name of the plant and its common everyday name. I watched with my mouth.

Back home where I came from, I knew the local names of the trees and plants. I never thought of what they are called elsewhere, let alone what their botanical names were. I recognized the hibiscus plant growing in a pot along the wall. It was not the purple one, though. I stooped to read its label. *Abelmoschus manihot* it said – the common name was the lilac hibiscus. I recognized the tomato plant too. Who would not? It was green. I never knew the botanical name of the green tomato was *Solanum betaceum*. In my school days, we were taught these names, but they never stuck. Maybe the only one that stayed with me all these years was the *Magnifera indica*, the botanical name for mango. Perhaps because it is magnificent, succulent, and sweet. Maybe because we had hundreds of mango trees growing along the River Nile. During the mango season, we spent lots of time in the gardens by the river.

The group coming after us almost pushed me down. I quickly moved along before they started creating a scene.

Towards the end of the building, we finally found the end of the queue and joined. We stood behind a family of three, a toddler in a stroller and little girl holding her father's hands. The mother was nowhere to be seen.

A man in front of the family was sweating profusely. He looked like he just ran the 20k marathon and never finished. He had his shirt tight on his waist. He raised his right hand to wipe the sweat from his forehead. A tropical bush growing under his armpit loomed largely.

The queue moved along some more.

"Why are we doing this again?" he asked.

She laughed sweetly.

"You don't want to change your mind now, do you?"

"I was just wondering loudly," he said. "Why does it smell like rotten meat. This plant?"

She told me before. I knew the answer too. The stinking plant does that to attract insects and flies for pollination.

She just looked at me.

"When are you leaving DC?" she asked instead.

She probably thought I was bored stiff. She felt it.

"I am still around and will not be leaving anytime soon," I said.

"Have you seen all the museums already?"

She was talking about the Smithsonian museums. The museums were actually not far from where we were on the Washington Mall. I had always wanted to see them. Three months in DC, and yet I had not even visited one. Shame.

"Not yet," he said. "I want to see all of them someday."

"You won't finish them in one visit, you know. I understand you can spend a whole day in one, and by the time you finished, you will not have the energy for a whole month to start the next one."

I laughed. I knew Lelisha was exaggerating. But who cared?

"I heard the air and space museum is cool. Maybe we could start there," I said.

She had a different idea.

"I am waiting for the Museum of African American History and Culture that will soon open," she said. "I want to see that. I have always wanted to learn more about the African American story. The museum will be my starting point. Do you know that it is the only one designed by an African? Isn't that sweet?"

I did not know.

Lelisha spoke like an audio version of the World Book Encyclopedia. That is what I loved about her. So intelligent and so knowledgeable.

"That is lovely," I said. "There are bound to be some awesome things in there."

The queue turned the corner of the building. The queue had already stretched further and further as more people joined. A couple came along. I could see that the lady with the pink hat was dejected.

"I don't think I could do this," the lady in the pink hat said glumly.

"At least it is moving," the man by her side said. "Let's hang in there for some time. It is the last day, and the bloom will fade tonight. We couldn't afford to miss this."

We moved along to join the back of the queue. Closer to the entrance, I saw the picture of the flower for the first time. It was displayed on the main supports of the airport style retractable belt barriers.

The picture had some writings on it: *What is so appealing about the corpse plant?* It was like they read my mind and wanted to put the question to rest. When she told me earlier that the corpse plant is blooming and she wanted to come to see it, it was the first time I heard of this plant. It stank like rotting meat when it bloomed, she had said. And that it will only happen again after ten years.

I thought it must be exciting. It got my interest, and here we were. The placard said the corpse flower is enormous in its natural habit, growing as tall as twelve feet. For effect and comparison, the blooming plant was shown against the silhouette of a man. It was taller than an average height man.

The door was closed just in front of us as a smaller group were admitted inside the building. We were about ten feet from the entrance. We waited. I was already itching to go see it. The flower that brought me all the way from Baltimore to see.

A notice on the board announced that the gardens will close at 11:00 pm, instead of the usual 5:00 pm. They were probably right in doing so, looking at the excitement and the crowd it had attracted. And this being the only night before the flower started dying, they had a point.

We waited some more.

Finally, the lady opened the door and ushered us in. We were handed another print with more details about the corpse plant.

It loomed in front of us as Lelisha, and I entered the main building.

The flower looked precisely as it was shown on the sheet handed to us at the door. It towered above our heads. The central spike protruded skyward – *Amorphophallus titanum*. The crowd surged forward as more people entered. The man with the bush under his armpit moved to the front, elbowing his way through the group. He looked impatient.

The glass canopy extended high up like a cathedral ceiling, allowing natural light to filter through the treetops into the room like in a dense jungle. The atmosphere was more humid. It had some tropical feel to it.

There was no smell, yet. I expected to be overwhelmed by the pungent odor of rotting meat, as was described.

"Do you smell anything," I asked her.

"Nothing. Maybe we should go up close."

There was nothing. Maybe the smell had already gone. Vanished. Evaporated. The plant dying. Perhaps the flower had already given out all the bad smell on its first day of blooming.

"Where is its natural habitat?" I asked.

"Indonesia."

"So, it doesn't grow anywhere else? It looked like it can grow in Africa. There are jungles and rain forests there that could be hiding these kinds of plants, you know. Like my back yard in the village."

"Trust me, if it is there, they would have found it."

"Have they looked everywhere? Africa is a vast continent. As recently as two years ago, they still find new species of animals and plants in Africa."

"I don't doubt that, but not this plant. The African climate is not suitable for its growth."

I gave up.

I took pictures of the plant. Lots of photos with my smartphone.

I could see the excitement in Lelisha's face as she took some pictures too. She talked and talked about how excited she was to at last see the corpse flower. I took photos of her in front of the flower; she looked like a model in a tropical paradise.

The excitement was too high for most of the people. Those who knew about the plant were more animated. As they tried to explain to the others around them who had no idea or never heard of it before.

The crowd moved away, already being asked to keep moving forward so that the people outside could get in too. Another group moved into the area as the door was opened for them. The room filled with a rejuvenated excitement of the newcomers.

Lelisha and I found our way out of the room where the corpse flower grew. I felt surreal like I had just viewed a dead body at a funeral home.

We went back to Union Station and sat at Starbucks. The sun had dimmed behind the low hanging clouds. More and more people found their way into the café, away from the heat. The main hall was dotted with travelers either hurrying inside towards the tracks or emerging towards the transit system area. Some travelers were just lounging on the seats in the central station hall.

Our orders arrived as we watched the station liven up with an impromptu performance by a group of African American teens – two boys and two girls. One of the boys placed a small DVD music player on the granite floor and cranked up the volume. A hip-hop music bellowed out of the small system. A small crowd formed around them as they danced, making some intricate synchronized moves. The group did a formation and started moving their bodies, arms out slanged like octopuses, and hips gyrating to the music. It is like they were auditioning for some weird music competition on another planet.

Once the music stopped, the lady with the tighter shorts placed a tin cup on the ground and asked the people to donate handsomely to their cause. She said something about raising funds for a summer school project in their neighborhood to support homeless kids.

Immediately some people moved away, looking disinterested. A few people dropped off some quarters that jingled loudly in the tin cup. Others placed dollar bills and moved on.

"That is a cause worthy of support," Lelisha said.

"There are too many of them. It is hard to decide what to support," I said.

"Just follow your heart," she said.

I took a ten-dollar bill out of my nearly empty wallet and walked across to the group and dropped it in the hat. When I returned, Lelisha was smiling, her face radiant and beautiful.

She held my hand and looked me in the eyes.

"Thanks for doing this with me today," she said. "You don't know how much this means to me."

"I am happy I can be here with you," I said.

I gave her a hug, my heart pounded like a mystic drum. The world around me disappeared for a second. I felt a new beginning had started, on the day I went to see a flower bloomed.

12
—

Seizures

IT IS HAPPENING.

Again.

I know it every time it does.

Especially at night.

The darkness in my room is broken by a thin ray of lighting coming out from the corridors outside through the slightly opened door.

The silence of the night is broken by a dull sound, a struggle. A noise of running feet. On the hard tile floors of our big house, it is deafening. Heavy running feet.

A thud.

Mummy and Daddy.

I know what it is.

Every time I know when it happens.

I pull the covers off my body and creep out of my bed towards the door. There is a frantic movement outside. Next door. I know the room next door is Rando's. My brother. He sleeps alone. Like me.

My stomach hurts. It feels like I have knots in there. Maybe it is from the food I ate last night. I never liked pasta anyways.

Slowly, I open the door and walk to the corridor. The light from Rando's room casts a long streak down the hallway. The entrance to his bedroom is half-open. I peep in without opening it further.

Mummy has Rando pinned to the bed, his body shaking violently. He is moaning. A sound that wakes me up every time it happens.

He has the fits.

Again.

Mummy struggles to keep his body from moving. I can see that she is also crying. Silently. Tears flow down her face. Daddy gets the needle ready. He puts it on Rando's thigh and injects him. He puts the needle away and helps Mummy in holding Rando down. Slowly Rando becomes quiet. His body stops moving. His breathing becomes heavy and labored.

Mummy slowly wipes some white materials from around Rando's mouth. She turns around her head and saw me standing there. I can feel that she is heartbroken. But her face is blank. She goes back to looking at Rando as he calmly sleeps. With her right hand, she rubs his head slowly, purposefully.

"Go back to your room," she finally says in a low voice.

I stand still without moving. The knot in my stomach tightens. I feel the pain going to my back and coming around. My stomach churns like there is a rat on a treadmill running inside. I once saw a rat like that at school. That is how I feel.

Maybe I need to go to the toilet.

"Will he be all right?" I asked.

"He is fine. Go back to sleep."

Daddy gets up from the bedside and comes over to the door. He takes me by my hand and leads me back to my room. The knot in my stomach tightens a bit.

I get into my bed, and daddy sits near me.

"I want you to know something, Anzo," he says. His voice is not the usual. He always talks to me. It sounds very foreign. Very far off. It is like I am listening to a different person. Not Daddy. "Rando has the usual fits. Again. I know you are worried, too, as we all are. He will be fine soon."

I close my eyes and just lay there. I cannot say anything. My eyes remain close as daddy continues to talk to me. His voice drifts far and far every minute. I cannot comprehend why it has to happen every day like that. Rando is my brother. My little brother. He does not deserve to be like that. To have to suffer like that.

My stomach hurts.

I worry.

Rando is not only a brother but also my friend. A very close friend. We go to school together. Have our lunches together and look out for each other. We walk back home together. Always. We are inseparable.

His fits have hurt his self-esteem. He is now withdrawn to himself and never ventures outside or make new friends. One incident has changed him wholly. Completely.

It was the beginning of the school year. We were at the assembly line. Our bright yellow shirts on dark khaki shorts shone in the early morning sun. The teachers were making sure we were standing in straight lines. One teacher was moving up and down the line, stick in hand. Our teachers are used to beating pupils with their sticks. On days like this, one has to be very careful about how you dress to school.

Some rules at school are not to be broken. Tuck in your shirts. Comb your hair. Cut your fingernails short. If you are found in violation of such rules, you are in trouble. Big trouble sometimes. Checking for long fingernails happens daily. The teacher walks down the line, every student stretches their hands out, palms down for inspection of nails. If your nails are long or unclean, you are hit with the stick on the spot.

Instantly. I never want to be in trouble. Rando and I are always ready. Mummy made sure we are prepared for school every day.

Rando's class was standing in the line several meters away. A neat formation. Like army troops or the new recruits, we sometimes see on TV. Suddenly there was confusion as the pupils move back and out of their line at one go. Then they made a circle, and were looking at something. Someone on the ground.

Our well-ordered parade lines broke up in confusion as the students piled to see what is going on. Some were getting on the back of each to get a glimpse of what is happening. I, too, moved closer and squeezed between two big boys and saw it.

It was Rando. He was on the ground, shaking and moving his limbs from the side. His head was bumping on the ground as a white foam start to pour from his mouth. The students were just watching. Nobody made a move. It was like they were stuck to the ground.

I ran to him and knelt beside him as I tried to calm him and stop his body from shaking. One teacher pushed through the students and helped me subdue his body. Teacher Andrew turned Rando's head sideways, as the convulsions seized his body and raked him from side to side. After a little struggle, he became calm again.

He opened his eyes and sat up slowly. His faced downcast, his school bag thrown down by his side. He wiped the dust from his shirt and shorts. He looked at me.

"What happened," he asked. His voice tremble, shaky.

"You fell."

"How did it happen?"

"The fits came back."

"Take him to the office," Teacher Andrew said.

I took his hands and pulled him. The students parted as I led him towards the teacher's offices. To have some rest. To recover. Since that day, he was never the same.

The sun is already shining through the window when I wake up. My stomach still churns. It is not as bad as the night before. I run to the toilet across from my room. My stomach opens like a broken water pipe. I feel my energy drain as water leaves my body in vast quantities. Maybe it has something to do with what I ate last night. It hurts badly. It feels like a tug of war is going on inside. I feel bad. I do not like stomach aches like this. I become sick, in pain, and continuously running to the toilet.

When I leave the toilet, I can hear voices in the living room. Voices of people I have not heard before. I cannot recognize any of the voices.

I found several people sitting in the living room. The room feels full. We never had so many people in the place before.

Rando sits in the chair by the door. His back is to me. Two or three men are standing by the window. Their voices become subdued as I walked in. My eyes are still sleepy; I cannot figure out who all the people were. I haven't seen any of them before. Never.

Mummy looks at me as I stand there, sizing up the people.

Daddy is nowhere to be seen.

"Come and sit down here," Mummy says.

"Hey, young man, how are you?" The person who speaks is standing by the wide window. His back was to me as I entered. I turn to see him facing me. I realize he is a pastor. His white-collar gives him away. He wears a black shirt and a grey jacket.

"What is your name?"

"Anzo," I say.

"Come here, Anzo. How old are you?"

"Ten."

"Ten," he echoes. His voice is the loud one I hear from my room. "I am Pastor Jeremiah. Nice meeting you, young man."

He shakes my hand.

I have not met Pastor Jeremiah before. The only pastor I know of is

Father Gregory, the white priest from Italy who runs the after-school programs at the church.

The other people gather around and sat down too.

"Let us congregate to start our prayers," Pastor Jeremiah says. "We have come to this house this morning to pray for our little son Rando that God will relieve him of his condition."

So that is the reason for their coming? To pray for Rando? Is it about last night? The fits?

The service goes on and on. He prays for the family. He lays his hand on Rando's head.

We stand up. They sing a song. We sit down again.

The pastor speaks some more. His hands gesticulating like a windmill. I dose off.

I have not been sleeping well for the last three nights. I know that because I have a stomach bug. My stomach rumbles at night when I turn in my bed. Or just when I am about to sleep, it pulls me from side to side. It feels like a tug of war is going on inside. And I have diarrhea. A bad diarrhea.

That night I dream about Rando and I playing on the school grounds. It is just him and me. Nobody else. We are playing with a new kite he receives from uncle John. He flies it; it rises higher and higher. He runs with it as I follow. He is laughing and running and laughing and running as the red, white and blue kite rises higher and higher. Suddenly, he floats in the air like the kite, his arms outstretched like an airplane.

13

Hotel Refuge

I PLAY FOOTBALL WITH MY FRIENDS EVERY DAY. WE PLAY IN THIS OPEN field near our house and have been doing so ever since we were much younger. We play after school. We play after doing chores for our parents. We play after working on the farms. We play during the holidays. We play when it rains.

It is fun playing football in the rain. We chase the ball. Our bodies become wet, and our clothes stick to our bodies. The ball becomes heavy. It does not bounce much. When you are hit on the head, it pains. It is a funny pain that makes your head spin, like you have malaria. But just a little turn, and you are back to the game. If you are not steady enough, you can fall on your head, and it will pain some more.

Jingi is my friend. One of my closest friends. A trusted friend. He brings his football to the field. His father brought the football from Khartoum. It is white and round and has black stars on it. It has numbers too. He says it is the year the World Cup was played in America. He said his father told him so. I do not know what year it was. I do not even remember when the World Cup was played in America. I only knew that the ball was brought to us from Khartoum, not America. Maybe it is true. Maybe it is not. Who can tell? I do not want to know.

Jingi and I live close to each other. He is my friend from way back. Jingi is a keen footballer. He is short, but not very short short. We call him Tong Tong. I am slightly taller than him. Jingi can run like a deer or a cheetah. His short legs can make him run fast, faster than any of us.

Our field is not even vast. Part of it is covered by grass, which can grow tall in the rainy season. Where the goalposts were, there is no grass. We have two long sticks for goalposts. A path has been created right through the field by people who used the short cut through our area. The field is small. Not the same size as a real football field. Maybe half of it. Maybe not. I do not think any of us have the strength to run the full length of the actual football field. Not any of us can. Our playing field is just right for us. For our ages.

When we get to the field, we line up and choose team captains. Then each captain selects his players in turns. I always get to choose my players. I am always the team captain for our side. I am a good footballer. Not many plays like me. Everyone wants to play on my team. We are always winners. Each time we play. We win. During our games, we have no referees. We do it ourselves. When someone commits a foul, we agree it is a foul, then the free-kick is given. A penalty is difficult to officiate. Sometimes we disagree, and no penalty is given. Of course, everyone wants to win.

Because we do not have jerseys, one team must remove their shirts and play bare chests. It is the norm. To decide which side should remove their shirts, the first team to concede a goal do that. Easy and no complaints. Unfortunately, sometimes we play for long without scoring. No one removes their shirts. If you pass the ball to the opponent by mistake, it is your fault.

We are not very many boys who always play there. But a good enough number for a game. The field has many memories. Some are good. Some are bad. The bad ones should be forgotten. Never to be told. I am not sure it is a good idea to remember those bad ones. Not good. I know one bad one that I can say to you. It is not so bad. It is not good either. But I will tell you.

It is the day Jingi broke his leg. You see, it is not bad. Like very, very bad. Yet it is not good. Not good to break a leg. Especially while playing football. Maybe not even any sport. But he broke his leg while playing football. It is bad. Jingi had the ball. He ran towards the goal. I think he slipped. Or hit a stone in the field. He fell. Badly. When we reached him, his leg was twisted. The front is looking backward. Like he is walking back yet going forward. He cries. He feels pain. It is bad. First, we run away from him. Because we have not seen anything like this before. Ever. No one has broken a leg in the fields before while playing football. It is something we have not seen.

When we returned to him, he was holding his leg. The twisted leg that is walking backward. He cries loudly. He was in pain. Horrible pain. I ran to his home to tell his father. He came back quickly, and they took him to the hospital. When we visited him the next day, we found him strapped in some materials. His leg was tied to a metal something. It was covered in white something. Some hard, white plaster wrapped around his leg. He smiles. He tells us it is no longer painful. They injected him with something to take away the pain. He told us. He smiled and joked and laughed and smiled some more. We were happy to see him like that. I mean, happy. Of course, we were not pleased to see him with a broken leg tied up to something like that. He did not play football with us for a long time after that.

Whenever we play football, some people come to watch us play.

Neighbors. Those passing by. Even some girls from school come sometimes. Just to watch us. We see them, and we play better. We run better. Do tricks. Dodge in style. Hit the ball with our heads. Or chest. Sometimes it will hurt, but you do not want to show it to the girls watching.

Because our group is small, we did not have matches with other teams much. Other boys play too. We have Zolo, who is our goal keeper. Perfect one. We have the Bongo twins. We call them Bongo One and Bongo Two. They are also excellent players. They look very much alike that it is difficult to tell them apart. They are our wingers, left and right. One time during the holidays, we asked Jing's father to write a letter that we take to the shops and ask for contributions from people to buy the jerseys and balls. A kind of fundraising. We do not want to rely on Jingi's ball. What will happen if it has a puncture and deflates? I know once we get the jerseys, I will wear number ten. It is a good number of great players.

One day we came to the field to play after school. Our area has been cordoned off. We found some men there. There were also big cars. Trucks. They have many things in them. We didn't know they were doing. The things they had in the vehicles. But they told us not to play there again. They said the field was now their property. We were shocked. How could someone just take our playing field? Just like that? When we wanted to get there, they blocked our ways and told us to find another place to play.

You see, there is no other empty spot to play football. The place next to the market has been built into a big house. It did not take very long to make it. Now there are many cars there. All the time.

Another place near the church is tiny to play football in. Some girls play volleyball there. Not always. Sometimes when we were tired of playing football, we go watch them. They are only girls. Boys say it is a girl's game. No boys play volleyball. If you go to play with them, you will be called soft. We just watch them for entertainment. And for other things.

When they play volleyball, the girls jump and shout and clap and tease each other. We particularly like to see them skip and jump. Jump high enough for us to see their exposed panties. They never notice. But whenever we see a glimpse of one of them, we shout the color. "There goes red," we cry out. They never notice that their panties show. Especially when they jump for the ball. That was fun. Their field is too small for us.

We are shut out of our own field. Our memories have been taken from us. It happens suddenly. But quietly. That is when we stopped playing football. Because our playing field has been taken away from us. The men put up a fence around our playing field. They closed it off. Put a security guard with a shiny new khaki uniform on the entrance. He does not carry a gun. Just a big stick to chase away when we come closer. We feel we can beat him. He has no weapon. He cannot shoot us. But we did not. There is no place inside any more to play in.

More cars came. Big trucks bring many kinds of stuff. Sand. Rocks. Bricks. We see them every time we pass by where we used to play football. More men join the place. Digging. Carrying soil. Other pieces of stuff. Many more things happened there.

"What are you doing here," we ask the security guard one day.

He did not chase us. We come slowly. Smiling so that he knows we are not afraid. But when he stands up, he has this stick in his hands. We fear. I want to run. But I cannot. Jingi holds my hand. If I run, I can run fast. I do not have any shoes. I can run away from him. But not today.

He looks at us. He knows we will not run away. He sees our faces. We smile.

He relaxes and goes back to sit in his chair by the door.

We stand by the gate.

He suddenly stands up and shouts at us.

"Move away from the gate. The truck is coming, you dirty boys. *Waskaneen.*"

We move to the side. The guard opens the metal gate. A truck goes in. It raises dust in the air. Jingi sneezes and coughs. His chest was bad in the past days. He coughs a lot at night, he says. The dust makes him cough again.

When the dust has gone, the security guard continues to look at us. He clears his throat and spit.

"They are building a hotel," he says.

"A what?" I ask.

"A hotel," he repeats. "It is a place where people can come, pay money and sleep."

Oh. I did not know a thing about hotels. Our house is not built like that. It is a tukul. Grass roof. Mud walls. That's all.

"Will we stay in it too?" Jingi asks.

"Not for you, villagers," the security guard says. "It is for rich people who have money. Do you have money? Do your parents have money?"

I want to hit him with a stone and run. He is very insulting. The security guard is. Maybe because we look dirty. Our clothes are not very new. Cloths from second-hand dealers in the market. He does not look rich himself. Yes, he is dressed up in khaki and a clean shirt. We walk away from him and go back to the house.

Because we no longer play football, we find other things to do. We go to the river. We play in the river for a long time. Swimming and diving and playing. There is a spot in which tree branched span over the water. We go climb the tree and dive into the river. After playing, we eat mangoes from the farm near the river. We do not pick from the trees. The watchmen in the garden will not let us. We collect those that have fallen on the ground. They are usually yellow and soft and juicy. Some are rotten. Smelly. But we always find good ones. Better ones.

We also spend time shooting birds in the bushes with catapults. We make our catapults from old bicycle inner tubes. The Y-shape stick we pick from the tree. We select the best ones so that they do not break. The part for putting the stone, we get it from old leather shoes. We fashion them nicely and use them. Good catapults make you shoot better. Get more birds faster.

Every day we pass by our old playfield, we see that the building is getting bigger and bigger. Days become weeks and months. A year passes by. It rises above the corrugated iron fence, it went above the trees near the edge of the field. It grows and grows. Now it is very tall. A tall building where we used to play football.

The workers then build a wall around it. We no longer see the inside. They paint its walls brown and white. It is the color of brown beans. Like the beans we used to eat at school. Big windows. Glass windows we see all around.

The building is finished. Colorful flags go up all around it. On the rooftops, near the main gate. Multiple flag poles along the side of the building. Many flags. Of different countries. A big signpost proclaims the name of the building, a hotel. When we pass it in the evening, the letters shine in the dark like a million fireflies pack into a glass pipe. A million stars twinkling.

We see new security guards. Three of them, at the same time. Always. They have small radios, these black objects with antennae sticking out of them. But the new guards still carry sticks too. What are they protecting with sticks? Jingi thinks he knows. He says because the people who come there now are rich, they need to be protected. New cars go in and out all the time. Brand new vehicles we have not seen before. Different types. Different colors come in and out of the big gate of the hotel. It is a strange place for us. A place too distant, yet close by. We can only imagine what the inside looks like. We can only dream up scenarios of how the rooms are like.

We paint our own pictures of ourselves at the hotel. We imagine ourselves arriving at the hotel. The security guard who used to chase us away, scramble to open the gate and salute with his right hand. I smile and wave at him. Bright lights everywhere as we go through the lobby. Someone dressed in a red uniform with lapels adorns in intricate designs, rushes over to take our luggage and show us to our room on the top floor.

We dream about a lot of things. Funny things. One day, Jingi says, we will be able to stay in the hotel. For now, it remains a dream. Our imagination.

It starts to rain. Heavy rainfall with lightning and thunder. I hate thunder. I shut my eyes when it happens. Boom. The sound hits me in the heart, like a thousand teacups breaking at once. We call it sagga, this dangerous thunder. It happens several times when I open my eyes. Then the flashes come too. Another thunder hits. The rain is pouring hard. It pours and pours, with no sign of stopping.

Jingi comes running to our house, drenched from head to toe. He looks like he had fallen in a ditch along the way. He is not happy. I can tell he has some fear in him.

"There is water in our house," he says. "It is flooded."

"How so?"

"Our house is underwater," he persists.

"How?" I ask you again.

I do not know why I ask again. I just want to ask. I want an answer. Maybe Jingi can tell me how.

"The water is coming fast," Jingi says. "This area will be underwater too."

I look around the compound. The rain continues. It falls and pours and runs down the side of the footpath near our house. I watch. Then it is no longer running. The water just stands there. Not moving, but more continue to fall. Heavy. Then flashes. And thunder once again. And flash and thunder, some more. We stand there and watch it falls.

The rain is not going to stop. I feel hopeless. Helpless.

It enters our compound and into the huts. We try to put old clothes around the door to keep the water out. Anything. This fails. It fills the inside of our huts. And it keeps rising. My small belongings start to float around the shelter. It has nowhere to go but up. And up it goes until we are deep in the water. We jump on the bed.

A loud noise follows as one of the huts collapses in the floodwaters. I feel fear immediately. Maybe the shelter we are in would collapse too.

"Let us get out of here," I say to Jingi.

As we wade through the rising water, a strong current push us towards the slope. We leave everything behind. Nothing we can do. Strangely the floods come at a time I am alone in the house. My father and mother have gone to the village. An uncle is supposed to come to stay with me in the house. He did not come because of the rain. And the flooding happening around us. Now our house is full of water.

We walk towards the hotel. The whole area around us is underwater. The road is now flooded. We cannot see where our steps are. We only follow by our knowledge of the road. Water pours toward our place. It keeps rising, reaching up to our hips. I hope they let us shelter in there.

I am soaked to my skin. The rains have stopped a bit. It gets colder.

I sit on the low ledge of the large glass window. I look at the cars parked outside. I cannot see further because the pouring rain makes a white blanket in front of my eyes. Sheets of white falling water. Since last night. Behind me is the large room. The security guard who let us in says it is the ballroom. My mind immediately goes to football. It is a room for holding wedding parties, he says.

Four other families are resting on the large soft mattresses provided. The families left their flooded houses behind. Each family is given a space in the corner. Each has four thick mattresses. And blankets. Clean blankets that still smell nice. Unused. Brand new. We have not slept in this kind of mattresses before. Our bodies sink as we lay on it. It curls around our bodies. Like a big hug. Jingi's family is asleep. It is still early morning.

We entered the building last night. We never expect to be accepted. Welcomed. It is all because of the rain which is still pouring. All last evening. It is the first time for us to enter the building. Right from the entrance, there is a thick carpet under our feet. We sink in with every step. We wash our feet before entering. They have us clean the mud from the rain first.

I have seen the building from the outside like an outcast. Forbidden from coming inside. The building is built on our football field. Now I know how it looks like from the inside. It is beyond our imagination. For today, it has become our refuge from the rains and floods and water. The hotel of our refuge.

14

Interstellar

I FLICKED THE SWITCH ON THE CONTROL CONSOLE. THE PERSONAL
Transport Vehicle, known as the PTV, went into autopilot and slowly
maneuvered to dock on the spaceship Z-Alpha, the largest spaceship in
the galaxy AFRX-10. The blue lights flashed, throwing a deep blue hue
inside the cramped space of the PTV cockpit. The PTV remained the
most reliable and fastest single-occupant vehicle, that covered the distance
from our planet Zetron to the spaceship at a mere fifteen minutes, down
from an hour in the previous generation of the transporter.

The PTV docked with a small thud and a shush. I shut it down
by pushing the cut off button. The pressurized cabin opened onto the
landing spot. I unstrapped myself, removed my helmet and stepped
out onto the ship. The docking crew whisked off the transporter to the
parking stations ten floors below.

I walked on the solid iron floor down the circular and tubular
corridor winding towards the control room at the center of the

spaceship. This early in the morning, the sun shone through the oval slits along the sides of the corridor. The spaces glowed, and the tiny fluorescent lights lining the sides shined like airport landing lights.

The first time I stepped on the spaceship was when I turned eight. In the colony, no children were allowed in the spaceship Alpha. At first, I thought the large letter "A" emblazoned everywhere on the ship and on the official gowns worn by the staff on the ship stood for the Alpha spaceship. I learned the true meaning much sooner than I had anticipated.

All eight-year olds, five hundred in number, were inducted in the colony that year. Dressed in overall suits and uniforms, we boarded the giant transporter from planet Zetron bound for the spaceship Z-Alpha. While on board, we were taken to a vast auditorium and spent the better of fifteen days every day being taught everything about our origins. Six in the morning to six in the evening. We slept in tiny cubicles but ate breakfast, lunch, and dinner in the auditorium.

It was fantastic learning about our origins. This was done by Deputy Paramount Chief Amollo. He told us we came from a planet that had died, known as Earth in a galaxy far, far away. Our part of that planet was known as Africa. Due to land misuse and misman-agement, the climate changed, and food became scarce. Through their interstellar voyages, they discovered the planet Zetron and migrated to it. When they returned to Earth several decades later, it was already wholly uninhabitable, and everything had vanished. We were shown pictures of the green countryside, mountain ranges, and flowing rivers that used to cover the Earth. There were beautiful cities and towns.

The A sign emblazoned on the spaceship sides, walls, uniforms, and equipment denoted Africa where we came from. It stood as a reminder of what we lost and left behind. It showed what happened to a planet due to its mismanagement and destruction by our activities.

It symbolized the continent we once lived on in the now disappearing planet Earth. Maybe one day, we might find ways to recreate the environment and return to the once glorious planet. Our induction and training were about hope, hope for the future.

The permanent displays of African scenery covered the walls on all sides. Images of the mighty Kilimanjaro mountain towered over lush green grassland, the white snow top looking like a cape. The animals that covered our land in the African continent, from the views of the Serengeti in what was East Africa, to the elephants along the Zambezi river, to the sprawling Sahara Desert with its numerous hidden secrets. The African big five took their positions on the walls – lion, elephant, rhino, buffalo, and leopard.

Several years later, I always got awed by the massive spaceship Z-Alpha at the geostationary location above planet Zetron. I walked towards the Central Control and Operations Room at the heart of Z-Alpha. It served as the heart and soul of the spaceship, where everything happened. The spaceship commander had the most central spot, sitting behind a massive steel desk and facing the large two meters high screen. A control monitor with many buttons sat atop one end of the counters to move pictures and feeds onto the large screen.

A line of computer banks and screens two levels below the central console received most of the feeds from the thousands of the small unmanned drones scoring the outer space. The central computer received the data at the processing unit and relayed them onto the central console.

Deputy Amollo swiveled in his chair and turned towards me as I stepped into the main cubicle. Two young officers worked on computers at the side of the large table.

"Welcome aboard, Junior," he said. He had a loud baritone voice. He stood at six feet five inches tall. He wore his full spaceship apparel, a flowing dark coat over his light blue trousers and shirt. The ubiquitous

A emblazoned his chest piece. He looked like he was readying himself for a battle. I wondered what action awaited me.

"Thank you," I answered. "You called me, sir."

"We have been receiving some weird signals from the direction of planet Makuria. It doesn't look like something we have seen before."

"So . . ."

"I thought you should see them. You are our number one analyst, remember?"

"You could easily have sent it through the network system."

"Well, we . . . I mean, I thought it is a good idea for you to come up here."

He pushed a small data tablet across the table towards me.

"We have all the data from the past several weeks in there," Deputy Amollo said.

I took the data tablet and turned to walked away.

"I also want to say I am sorry about your Dad. We all are."

"Dad is not dead," I shouted at him. My voice reverberated across the great hall. The two officers stopped what they were doing, stunned.

"I did not say that. It is over six months, and we have not heard anything from him. The drones have not picked any signal from his space craft."

The two officers got up and left the cubicle. Deputy Amollo had always been getting on my nerve. There always was something about him that irritated me so much. It was not his physique, which looked like he was a cross between an obelisk and centaur. It was not his voice either – the boring baritone voice.

"He will be back. I know he will. Dad will be back." I said slowly. My heart started beating faster like a mystic drum.

I walked out of the control room and headed towards my cubicle office in the far end of the long winding corridor. I needed time to myself. I had not been thinking of him lately. I thought by not talking or thinking about him, he may miraculously appear one day.

One of the young officers from the cubicle appeared and walked beside me.

"Junior, I am also sorry about your Dad," he said. "I know it may not be appropriate but I have something for you."

"What is it, Mansho?"

"Keep walking. Deputy Amollo is not telling the truth. There is something I like you to see."

Mansho slipped a data card in my hand. He turned into a corridor and entered a side door.

Dad served as the Paramount Chief and Captain of the spaceship Z-Alpha for the last twenty or so years. He was the two hundred and thirtieth chief to ascend to the position since the relocation of our people to Zetron more than two hundred years ago. He succeeded Paramount Chief Lotole III. As a trained engineer, he also served in the innovation's division, supporting the young engineers working on new ideas and programs for the spaceship Z-Alpha and planet Zetron. They were testing a new type of spaceship landing vehicle with new capabilities in terms of speed, maneuverability and stealth mode. It was known as Namsa II, after a former Paramount Chief of Zetron.

He had perfected the design and all the crucial segments himself. After several tests within the engineering workshop and the air tunnel, Dad decided to take the new proto-type space vehicle for a spin around the galaxy. He had not returned since.

I remembered the day perfectly. We all stood in front of the big screen in the control room. The small team of mission control staff for the new space vehicle were huddled around their consoles and small screens making final touches to the mission launch as zero-hour approaches.

Dad worked out of the fitting room with three members of his crew and climb into the space vehicle. We could all see this from the big screen. After they were strapped in, the camera zoomed out and we saw the whole ship. Namsa II was a beautiful ship. It had been kept a secret right from inception. Dad did not even speak about it at home. No one had seen the full-size spacecraft except for the engineers working on it from a secluded workshop.

Deputy Amollo oversaw the launch from the control room.

"One minute to launch," he beamed into the microphone.

After that, a clock started counting down. My heart tightened as I watched the space vehicle come to live and the lights blinked on its side.

"Ten seconds," a female voice said over the speakers. Then the voice continued to count down. "Nine, eight, seven, six, five, four, three, two, one . . ."

"You are on your way, Namsa II," Deputy Amollo said.

Namsa II floated off the launch bay and into the atmosphere around Z-Alpha and sailed off at a supersonic speed into the darkness.

Mission control monitored their progress, as Namsa II sent back data about its progress. The test ride took them past the planet BX-Atom and into the atmosphere around its solitary moon Tutu. They spent one month, testing the new equipment onboard and all its communication and computer systems.

On the day they were to perform the last test and head back to Z-Alpha, all communications with the spaceship were lost. All emergency signals were suddenly lost like there was an explosion. The engineers tried all they could to restore connection but to no avail. It seemed there was no hope of them returning.

Now this young engineer said the reports were not true.

Where are you Dad? What happened to your Namsa II?

I inserted the data card into my mini laptop and the program immediately went into secure mode with the firewall. No one would see what I was doing. As the system opened the data, the information streamed on the small screen. I realized immediately that these were raw data, unfiltered. No one on the spaceship could visualize the raw data received from the thousands of drones out there in the interstellar spaces. Not even me. What we got were filtered and pre-analyzed data to work on.

I hooked up the laptop to my UX Box, the Ultra-Data System Analytics, known as the UUDSA, and pressed the enter key. During the analysis, the screen showed crisscrossing shapes, cubes and circles and multi-colored triangles.

After one minute a summary appeared on the screen. I transferred it onto a larger screen on the side of my cubicle office. It showed that the source of the signal was coming from a location not far from planet K-Lock. It zeroed in on an area of about fifty thousand square kilometers. Too large. I reviewed the last known location of Dad's spaceship. It was within the zone. I checked the date stamp: 20 January 2320.

The crew were sitting on a data for the past four months and nobody told me about it? I knew Dad was alive out there. I always knew. But why was someone hiding the information from me, from most of us? Has Deputy Amollo had something to do with it? Someone was hiding the data. However, I knew who to talk to.

The giant unmanned K-9 supply ship docked at exactly nine in the morning. These ships come up every month to supply the spaceship Z-Alpha with food and water and other necessary supplies. The engineers had installed three floors to be used for gardening and storage, which could reduce dependency on supplies from planet Zetron.

I found my uncle Damaris supervising the final unloading of the K-9 supply ship at the docking bay.

SACRIFICE & OTHER SHORT STORIES

"Junior, good to see you," he said. "How have you been?"

"I am doing great, uncle Damaris," I said. "I would like to talk to you for a minute."

He turned to give instructions to his assistants. The two men listened attentively to his directives and left.

"Let's go back to my cubicle," he said.

I followed him through a small door into a slightly dark corridor. The passage wound through the different sections of the spaceship, with wide glass windows on either side throughout. We passed the room where the engineers checked the vehicles before being carried off for parking after each trip. Down the corridor, we came across the room where several small boys practicing judo and doing yoga. I could see them in their white garments, with the now universal emblem on the back.

"What is bothering you?" Damaris asked, when we got to his office. He had a much larger office than mine. It was in one of the corners of the spaceship, had two wide windows to look out into the open space far away. From here we could see the PTVs coming to dock in the several bays below us. It had enough space to dock up to twenty PTVs at once. On most nights, you could see shooting stars spray the sky with a splash of bright lights.

"It is about Dad," I said. "What new information do you have about his disappearance?"

"We have no new information. You know all that I know. I had briefed you about the searches, the efforts to pick up signals form their ship. Everything."

"Everything?" I asked.

"Yes, everything," he answered. "What are you alluding to? Is there something I don't know you want to tell me?"

I debated in my mind how to approach it. Uncle Damaris would have known if there were additional information. There would be no reason why he shouldn't share with me what he had learnt. After all, he should be as worried as everyone else, maybe, even more because it was about his brother. Maybe he was being kept in the dark too. It was possible.

"I don't know how to phrase it but there is new information about Dad," I said.

"What information?" he asked.

I gave him the printout from the data analysis I did on the card Mansho gave me. He looked at it and remained quiet, studying every little detail on the paper. His face registered nothing. Maybe, I was expecting more reaction from him, even a little, of joy, at least.

"I was told the last communication picked up from Dad's spaceship was five months ago. This data showed that they received some signals from the spacecraft three months ago," I added, when I did not hear anything from him.

"Where did you get this from?" he asked.

"Someone left it in my cubicle with a note. It said they received new information, but no one is talking about it,"

"It is my first time to see this. I will double check with the Deputy and let you know. If they are keeping it under wraps, it means someone doesn't want you and me to know."

"But why would someone keep this a secret? I have the right to know."

"Exactly, Junior. I will let you know what I come up with. Be careful and don't share the information with anyone."

I left his office and returned to my cubicle.

The Zetron Colony Council convened in the board room two floors above the main control room, enclosed in a thick bullet-prove glass. One could see the main control room from the board room. It had a massive round-table, with sitting for twenty-four members of the council. In front of every chair was a microphone and a touch screen, on which displays of the meeting and voting took place. The high cathedral ceiling melted into the sides two floors above. Natural lights came in from the high windows.

I sat two seats from Deputy Amollo and across the table from uncle Damaris. Dad's chair stayed empty, like it had been for the last five months. It remained an ominous sign of his unknown location. The fate of the Namsa II spacecraft and the entire crew remained unknown.

Deputy Amollo called the meeting to order and went through the agenda: reports from the different departments and sections, the engineers, the explorers, the food security teams, the power generation team. Each member of the council around the table had responsibility in one specific area. They made comprehensive reports, we discussed options and provided recommendations. The hours went by.

At last, my turn came. I took the report I developed earlier and flick the switches in front of me. The screens went live. Although each person could follow from their small screens, the report was also projected in the large screen. I took them threw the analysis I did, and explained all the signals that had been received so far.

"The bottom line is we don't know the sources of the signals yet," I dropped the bombshell.

The room went silent. I could only hear the hum of the computers. Nothing else. The Councilors looked at me for answers.

I continued, "we still don't know what produced the signals. Our drones have not spotted anything yet. It could be a new type of space vehicle or technology we don't know. We shall keep monitoring."

"Keep us updated," one councilor said. "I don't want to be in the dark. If it is a force from outer space, we need to be ready to confront it."

"Certainly, Councilor," Deputy Amollo said. "All units should be on alert; we shall meet every day from tomorrow until we know what is going on. Thank you, Junior. Meeting closed."

Before I could leave the room, an elated voiced boomed over the intercom. Deputy Amollo requested in the Control Room. I believe we just picked a signal from Namsa II.

We rushed from the board room, down the windy staircase to the main console. Deputy Amollo led, followed by uncle Damaris and I took up the rear.

"Bring up the signal on the screen," Deputy Amollo ordered. "What have we got here?"

"We are receiving a strong signal from a spacecraft. It seems to be one of ours."

"Do we have drones in the area?"

"Yes. One will be approaching the site in the next five minutes, sir,"

The five minutes felt like an hour, or two. Deputy Amollo stood on the central control area. He looked pensive. He had a faraway look and did look like he was in deep thought. My uncle Damaris remained two steps behind Deputy Amollo.

We are there in the next five seconds, four, three, two, one.

The big screen lighted up as the cameras on the drones came to live. The whole room gaped. There was no doubt at all that the spacecraft on the screen was Namsa II.

"Deploy the retrieval system," Deputy Amollo bellowed.

The retractable arm proceeded to attach to the spacecraft. Slowly, they moved as the drone pulled the spacecraft.

It was two weeks later before Dad, Paramount Chief Rukamansa, was well enough to sit in the council meeting. He stayed ten days in the hospital ward, recovering from weakness resulting from more than six months of hibernation. After the systems on Namsa II failed and all communications were cut off with the control room, they resorted to internal hibernation and drifting in outer space. The spacecraft was equipped with hibernation capsules that could last one year. It was sheer lack that one of the communication equipment suddenly came to live and started transmitting.

It was still unclear what happened to Namsa II. How could the new spacecraft just shut down during the flight? How could such a thing have happened? Was it a technical failure? Sabotage? Intentionally done, but by whom? And how? The questions were endless. The answers though were not forthcoming.

At the initial review, Dad reported that the flight was flawless. The new spacecraft functioned smoothly as they tried the new functionalities. They passed through space for two days and sailed further and further away from the mothership spaceship Z-Alpha. They sent back data to the control room. It was then that something abruptly happened that shut down the system.

The scientists reviewing the data from Namsa II came back with the shocking news.

"We are certain a virus was installed into the system prior to the launched. We are trying to ascertain how and who did it," the chief scientist said.

"So, there was a breach in the system," Deputy Amollo said.

"Yes, sir. We are working on trying to determine the source."

"We need to know sooner," Dad said. "I believe someone deliberately did it to have us killed. This is treasonous."

Dad and Deputy Amollo called me into the operation room one day. The data I analyzed was critical and it showed another dimension. It seemed a group of spaceships were headed towards us. A reconnaissance drone had approached the ships but before it could do much, it was shot down. It seemed an invasion of our planet was in the offing. From another planet.

They also told me that uncle Damaris had disappeared from his cubicle and one of our PTVs went missing, presumably he took it. I was shocked.

"Why would he do that?" I asked.

"My son, your uncle has betrayed us to the enemies," Dad said slowly. "We have found evidence that he planted the virus to destroy Namsa II. He had been communicating with the group that is approaching now. It seemed he wanted to take over this colony."

"How could he do that?"

"My brother Damaris has always wanted to be the Paramount Chief when our father died. He was not happy when he was passed over for the position. He has never forgiven me for that."

I was baffled. I had shared with him my findings about the data received and the possible finding of Namsa II. How could he do that now?

"He has defected to side with the approaching spaceships," Dad said. "We have nothing more but to fight back and keep our sovereignty."

I knew that the battle was going to be decisive when I got back to my cubicle. Spaceship Z-Alpha was put on full alert and all staff moved to their battle stations. Dad against his brother.

Reviews of *Sacrifice*

These stories are reminiscences of the past, a mixture of rural and urban life, of a glimpse of a life lived in Khartoum during the liberation war, and how that impacted on the life of war weary South Sudanese. With South Sudan's independence in July 2011, there is a modern trajectory in early city life, with metropolitan Juba city fast becoming a hotbed of con-people and other crimes. There is a sprinkling of a story which transports the reader to America, yet this is not the typical "Lost Boy" narrative. This is a tapestry of traditional story telling.

Victor Lugala, South Sudanese creative writer

The collection of fourteen interesting stories not only peeks into the lives of some ordinary South Sudanese during certain periods of their history, but also explores more universal themes. The experiences of the characters reveal significant tribulations and glories of varying degrees. Some of the story lines are direct, but most have twists and surprising endings, narrated with great skill.

David L. Lukudu, South Sudanese writer

www.ingramcontent.com/pod-product-compliance
Lightning Source LLC
Chambersburg PA
CBHW030435120726
47903CB00003B/979